PRINCE OF
BOOK ONE OF THE SO

Robert Ryan

Cover Design by www.damonza.com

ISBN-13 978-0-9942054-7-6
(print edition)

Trotting Fox Press

Contents

1. Murder and Mayhem

Nightborn. The sound of the name was bitter in Gil's ears. It was what the other boys called him, and he did not like it. Worse, he knew that he was about to hear it again. But he would not let that stop him from doing what he had to do.

For a little while he had watched as Elrika, daughter of the palace baker, struggled to fend off the sword strokes of the group that had set upon her. It did not matter that they were only wooden practice swords – they still hurt. Welts had risen on her skin, and a cut on her forehead dribbled blood toward her eyes. Bravely, she brushed it away with the back of her wrist and tried to defend against multiple attackers.

This was meant to be a sparring session. It was supposed to be one against one. But it was more violent than it should have been, and when the leader of the boys, older than everyone else, had nodded for his friends to join in it had suddenly become very personal. They all hated Elrika, for she was a commoner and they were of the aristocracy. It did not matter that her father owned baker shops scattered throughout the city and was richer than most of their own parents. She was not of the blood as they were, and they despised her for it.

Dust rose about their feet as the girl gamely dodged and turned, trying to fend them off. And she was good too. Very good. That infuriated them even more. She was nearly their match, but she tired beneath the hot afternoon sun and the constant blows that came from all sides no matter how fast she twisted and spun.

Gil glanced at the Swordmaster. The man watched from where he sat on a padded chair, slowly smoking his pipe. He had done nothing to intervene. The Swordmaster was of the aristocracy himself, and had inherited the position from his father twenty years earlier. No, he had done nothing, and it did not look like he was going to. He was a baron, and his sympathies lay with the boys rather than the daughter of a baker.

Elrika stumbled and the attackers struck her hard several times. She fell, rolled, and came to her feet again in one motion. The boys were surprised, and then laughed. But soon they moved in on her again.

Gil had seen enough. "Stop!"

The boys turned to him, and the eldest, their leader, sneered.

"Stay out of this, *elùgrune*. Or you'll be next."

There it was. Elùgrune. The old word for nightborn, but the voicing of the insult did not intimidate Gil. Instead, it filled his veins with fire. Still, he controlled his temper.

"The task we were set," he said calmly, "was to spar one on one. This isn't fair."

One of the other boys, emboldened by the ringleader's insult, took it further.

"Go back into the dark, elùgrune. Go back to whatever black pit spawned you."

They all laughed at that. Gil, the fire in his veins starting to throb, did not answer. He breathed slowly to try to calm himself, but they mistook his silence for fear, and that emboldened them even more.

Elrika seemed forgotten, and they turned on him. The eldest boy pushed him. It was not a hard push, but it sent Gil back a few paces. Still, he did nothing. He did not want to fight them.

The taller boy pushed him again, much harder this time. Then the other boys lifted their wooden practice blades and yelled insults. They were working themselves up to what must surely come next.

Gil glanced once again at the Swordmaster, but the man just sat there puffing smoke, staring at them all coldly with heavy-lidded eyes.

A thought flashed through Gil's mind when he looked back to the boys. He remembered the advice of Brand, his *real* teacher. *Go for the leader first when confronted by a group. He's the one who gives spine and willpower to the others.* It had been just like that here. Gil could almost hear Brand's voice continue. *Often, the many can be defeated by the destruction of the one.* That, Gil realized, was what Elrika had done wrong. She had tried to fight them all at the same time.

The ringleader went to push Gil once again, but just as he made contact Gil rocked his weight back a little and turned to the side. The older boy was suddenly pushing at nothing, and he was off-balance.

Gil struck. He did not use the blade of the wooden sword, but rather the rounded pommel. With a crack, he thrust it hard against the back of the other boy's head.

The ringleader dropped, his legs seeming to lose the ability to hold any weight, and he collapsed like a felled tree. Gil felt panic rise within him. A blow to the back of the head could be lethal, and he had struck harder than intended.

He did not look back though. With a leap he was among the other boys, but they scattered from him like leaves blown on the wind. Only Elrika stayed where she was, an intense look on her face that he could not interpret.

He heard a movement behind him and turned. The ringleader was struggling to his feet. His face was red with anger or shame, and blood dripped from his nose. He had fallen face-first onto the ground.

With a shaky movement the boy used the back of his hand to wipe the blood away. "Elùgrune!" he said, and his voice was a hiss of hatred. "Nightborn! Born of the blood of a witch! You'll pay for—"

He got no further. Gil struck again, this time a swift blow with the heel of his left palm. It caught the other under the chin and sent him sprawling backward onto the ground once more.

Quickly, Gil darted forward and kicked the sword out of his opponent's limp hand. Then he whipped around to face the other boys, but they had not moved.

His heart thudded in his chest, and his anger threatened to break loose. He almost went for the other boys even though they now made no move against him, and they saw that look on his face and feared it. They backed further away.

With a long breath he steadied himself and stayed where he was. His anger was no longer directed at them. He was seething at the insults that had been cast at him. *Elùgrune. Blood of the witch.* He had heard them all his life, but no one had ever explained to him exactly what they meant. That would change, and soon, he decided.

At last, the Swordmaster came over. For all that he sat through most of the training sessions on his cushioned chair, he was not that old. He walked over briskly, and anger distorted his face.

"Fool!" he said, stopping directly before Gil. "This was a sparring session, not a fight!"

"But they were—"

"Enough! You should be ashamed of yourself. In all my years, I've never met such an arrogant boy. Do you think you can get away with this? Do you think Brand will protect you? I don't care that he's regent. In this practice yard, I rule."

Elrika stepped forward. "Sir, he was only trying to help me." She paused, seeing the look on the Swordmaster's face.

"Be silent. I'll deal with you later."

He turned back to Gil. "Apologize. Apologize now."

Gil glanced behind him. The boy he had hit was standing once again, but he did not look well. No, not well at all. But he had deserved everything he had received, and Gil made his decision.

He faced the Swordmaster. "No."

The man looked as if he were about to fly into a rage. "What do you mean, no? No one says no. Not here. Not you. Least of all you!"

"By no, I mean no. I won't apologize. They were picking on Elrika. They could have hurt her, and you did nothing to stop them. So I did."

"It's not your place to stop anything boy!"

Gil held his ground. His heart pounded more than it had in the fight, but he was not going to back down. Right was right, after all.

The Swordmaster glared at him coldly. "I won't have my authority or my actions questioned. You're expelled. There's no place for you in this practice yard. You may go now."

Gil looked at him. He thought about arguing, but that would be pointless. Then he caught the hint of a smirk on the Swordmaster's face. Finally, he understood. The man had set him up for this. The whole thing had been a trap, and like a fool he had fallen into it. The aristocracy hated him even more than they hated commoners, but for a different reason.

There was no help for it now. He had done what he had done, and he was not sorry. He turned to walk away, but the Swordmaster was not quite done.

"Be sure to tell Brand exactly why you were expelled. If he doesn't understand, he can come here and I'll explain it to him personally."

Gil did not answer. He kept walking, but he *did* wonder how he was going to explain this to Brand. That was not something to look forward to.

He thought about Brand as he walked to the palace. Brand was regent, taking the place of the king who had once ruled the great city of Cardoroth. There were many stories about him. So many, and all hard to believe, yet they were still true. Gil was old enough to remember some events himself, or at least to have heard about them from people who had been there. And he had learned more as he had grown older.

Brand of the Duthenor, they called him. He had come from a wild tribe that lived in the wilderness far to the west. Quickly he had risen in the ranks of Cardoroth's army, and he had won the king's favor for feats of bravery that made other men tremble.

But it was not for bravery alone that the king had kept promoting a stranger. It was for his loyalty as well. Brand's word was his bond, and not once had he failed the king, either in a matter of trust or of courage. Gil knew that for a fact, because the king had told him so himself. The king, after all, was his grandfather. He had always spoken in the highest terms of Brand.

Gil walked ever more slowly. The more he thought about it, the more he worried about telling Brand of his expulsion. It was Brand himself who had sent him to study under the Swordmaster, and the last thing Gil ever wanted to do was disappoint him. Brand was in many ways like a father to him.

8

His own father was dead. His mother was away on a long journey, and Brand was his guardian. In a way, Brand filled in for his parents just as he filled in for his grandfather.

His grandfather was old. Old, and weary after long years of hard service. Only the wit and military strategy of that man had kept his realm's many enemies at bay. Cardoroth only existed today because of the old king, and Gil was proud of him.

But even great men wearied. The old king had served most of his life, and he had suffered greatly under the strain of incessant attacks to the city from without, and constant treachery from within. With only a few years left to live, he had made his most trusted and competent servant regent. Regent for his only heir, Gil himself. But no one asked Gil what he thought about all of that. There were lots of things they never asked him.

He slowed even further, dreading his return to the palace in shame. At least his grandfather would not know of this. He had left the city, trusting Brand implicitly. Where he had gone, no one knew for sure. But he was with his wife, Gil's grandmother, and Gil did not begrudge the short happiness they would have together, free of troubles, even if he missed them terribly. After what they had endured in Cardoroth, they deserved that.

Gil let out a long sigh. He should have seen through the Swordmaster's scheme. If there was one thing the aristocracy hated more than a foreigner being made regent, it was a prince too young to ascend the throne. For though Gil was of the aristocracy, here now was their chance to try to maneuver one of their own families into the kingship. They would have to be bold to do that, but the attitude of the Swordmaster showed they were capable of it. Still, Brand would never let that happen.

9

Gil walked through the palace gardens. The well-tended grounds were lush with new growth and flowers, and the hot afternoon sun burned above. It was a beautiful day, but more and more he dreaded telling Brand what had happened. Brand was many things to him – regent, hero, warrior. But most of all he was a tutor. Brand taught him as a father might a son, and the way of the blade, of combat and military strategy, was the least of it. Brand taught him how to be a king, and how to defend himself and the realm that one day he would rule. That knowledge was needed too, for both he and Cardoroth had many enemies.

All of these were good reasons that the old king had made Brand regent. But he still missed his grandfather. And now his mother also, who had left to visit with his grandparents. She knew where they had gone, even if she would not tell.

Out of habit, he looked about him as he walked through the gardens. Sure enough, he caught glimpses of the bodyguards who trailed him wherever he went. It was proof that he had enemies, and it made him uncomfortable.

At last, he entered the palace and walked freely through its halls. He knew where he was going, could have found his way blindfolded if he had to. He had grown up here, and he had long since discovered and explored its every nook and cranny.

He knew exactly where he was going now – the throne room, even if he did not really wish to. But, at this time of day Brand would still be there, though the official audience period was finished.

He came to the great doors, which stood open. There he paused a moment, and though he did not see them he sensed the bodyguards, much nearer now, behind him. They paused also.

He did not wait long. It would not do to let anyone see his hesitation. So, with a brisk step he entered the throne room.

His steps echoed loudly. The marble floor was white and polished, and his boots made a slapping sound against it that he could not hush. Worse, the vaulted ceiling that rose to a dizzying height seemed to swallow the sound and then cast it back a thousandfold.

He saw Brand straightaway. There was a woman with him, old and gray-haired, but her eyes were very sharp. The two of them appeared to be finishing a conversation. The stranger gave Brand a bow, gathered some papers, and left. She did not look at Gil on her way out, but he sensed no animosity.

Gil approached the regent, but despite himself his pace slowed. Brand looked as he always did. He was dressed in well-fitting, but rather plain clothes. They were of the same sort that ten thousand other men might now be wearing on the streets of Cardoroth. And Brand's physical appearance was the same – ordinary.

The regent was not tall nor short. He was, perhaps, a largish man because his muscles were well-developed and could be discerned even beneath his clothes. But if so, it was no more than any laborer in the city. About his every move was a sense of lithe alertness, as though he could transform from stillness to sudden action quicker than the eye could follow, but that too was not unique. It was the look of a warrior, and there were many such in a city long beset by enemies.

But then Brand turned his blue eyes upon him, and as always Gil sensed the raw charisma that set him apart. Here was a man of power. Here was a man who commanded by inspiration, trust and loyalty. Here was a man who looked into the hearts of others and saw their strengths and weaknesses – saw, forgave, and encouraged.

11

Here was a man warriors would follow to death. *Had* followed to death, and that the people of the city loved even if the aristocracy did not. Here was the man who had been the city's greatest hero in the recent war. Cardoroth would have fallen if not for him, and even though Gil had not been old enough to fight, he had heard firsthand from his grandfather exactly what Brand had done.

Gil made up his mind. Brand was not the sort of man you lied to, or even tried to present yourself to in a favorable light. You just told him the truth. He respected that, the good or the bad, and the consequences of Gil's actions would be … whatever they would be. He took a deep breath and accepted that.

Brand raised an eyebrow. "You're back from training early. What happened?"

There it was. Straightaway the man knew something had happened. Not much ever slipped past him.

Gil looked him in the eye. "I'm sorry. The Swordmaster expelled me."

There was a pause. A flicker of emotion played across Brand's face, but Gil did not think it was surprise. Had he already known?

"It seems you've had an interesting day. Tell me all about it."

So, that's what Gil did. He told Brand everything. He held nothing back, including his fear that he had struck the other boy too hard on the back of the head, and his relief that the boy had stood up afterward.

Brand asked some simple questions, then finally shrugged.

"I see no fault in what you did."

Gil was amazed. He had been expecting some kind of punishment.

Brand looked at him curiously, evidently sensing his surprise.

"It's a case of properly attributing causes and effects," he explained. "You did the right thing. Some would argue that you should have tried harder to reason with the other boys. Truth is, though, some people can't be reasoned with. This was one of those situations. The other boys were always going to do what they were doing. The only question was, what were you going to do about it? In the end, you may have saved Elrika from serious injury."

Brand leaned back in his chair. "The effect of being expelled was beyond your control. Just because a man tries to do the right thing, it doesn't follow that the end result is good. So, it's not the end result a person should be judged by – it's the intent they started with."

Gil was startled. He had never thought of things in that light before. Brand was always opening his eyes to other ways of seeing things.

"Well, I'm glad you think so," Gil said. "I still feel bad that I was expelled though. Word of that will get around the city, and not everyone will see things as you do."

Brand considered that. "What matters more is that you know the truth. You can't worry too much about other people. As for being expelled, well, the Swordmaster overstepped his power there. Go to training tomorrow as normal. I'll send Lornach with you so that there'll be no trouble."

Gil was surprised all over again. He had not expected that, and he had no desire to see the Swordmaster at all, but if Lornach was going to be there then he had nothing to fear. In fact, he could hardly wait to see the look on the Swordmaster's face. Lornach had a way of dealing with these sorts of situations. It would prove memorable. Then he remembered something, and suddenly felt less buoyant.

"The other boys called me elùgrune again," he told Brand. "Am I? Is what they say true?"

Brand straightened in his chair. Once again there was a flicker of emotion, but it was gone before Gil could read it.

"Let no one tell you who you are," Brand answered. "You are the sum of your own thoughts and your own actions. The first becomes the second, and the labels of other people are meaningless. At least, unless you give them power yourself. Remember that."

Gil held out his hands. "Then what do these marks really mean? No one ever answers that properly."

Brand did not even look at the marks, the two small dots of white skin, like eyes. They had been there all Gil's life, were a part of him. But they made him different from everybody else, and he did not know why. Brand had seen them before. So had the boys at the practice yard. It was from that moment that they had begun taunting him. Again, he did not really know why.

With a shrug, Brand leaned back.

"If you're old enough to ask the question," he said, "I think you're old enough to know the answer. The Camar people, that great race who swept out of the west and came east to form cities and realms, including Cardoroth, tend to think of the sign of Halathgar – a constellation of two stars like eyes, just like the marks on your palms, as a sign of sorcery. In Cardoroth, that mark is known as the Seal of Carnhaina."

That much Gil already knew. He knew what the marks were called, and he knew that Queen Carnhaina was his distant ancestor. He could not quite remember how long ago her reign was though, perhaps as much as seven hundred years.

Brand went on. "What you have probably also heard is that Carnhaina delved into sorcery. So, in Cardoroth, the constellation of Halathgar is associated with dark magic.

14

She took the constellation as her own sign, and also as her royal seal."

Gil held his palms before him and studied them. The marks on each hand were pale, more or less white spots devoid of any pigment. They were not quite round, and indeed looked like eyes, especially when he held both hands together. But all of this he had already been told before, if not quite so directly.

"Then what people have said all my life is true. Ultimately, I'm born from a witch." He could not make himself say anything about the words nightborn or elùgrune.

Brand scratched his chin. "Well, many in Cardoroth would say so."

"And what do you say?"

"I say this. Maybe the sign of Halathgar, or the Seal of Carnhaina – call the mark what you will, represents dark magic. But among my own people, among the lands of the Duthenor, there's a different view."

This was something Gil had not heard before. Brand rarely spoke of his homeland, so Gil listened closely.

"I remember my father taking me for a walk one evening. I was younger than you are now. Far younger, but I remember it clearly. It was a cold night, and still. It was also very late. Frost lay in the hollows, and the stars were piercing bright. We came out from beneath the night-shadow of a great oak, and he pointed suddenly to the glittering sky. 'See, my son! Bright Halathgar shines upon us!'"

Brand paused, seemingly lost in memory. Gil knew that his father must have died not long after that night, for it had happened when Brand was quite young. It brought back memories of his own father's death, and he suddenly felt very close to this unusual man.

Then Brand, almost imperceptibly, straightened in his chair.

"My father told me then that the constellation was a sign of good luck. From then onward, I look for it every time I go out into the dark. But you, Gilcarist, need never search it out. You will carry it with you all the days of your life."

Gil felt suddenly very strange. He also wondered why Brand had used his full name. Come to think of it, Brand *did* do that quite often. It made him feel as though he were being treated as an adult, and he liked that.

Unexpectedly, Brand went on. He obviously had more to say on the subject, and Gil was fascinated.

"But, truth be told, there's an older meaning than either the Camar or Duthenor really know."

Brand paused, considering his words. Gil remained perfectly still. The great hall was silent and brooding, as though it too listened.

"The constellation of Halathgar has an ancient significance. The immortal Halathrin call it the Lost Huntress. To them, it's a sign of surpassing good luck. The legends they tell about it are among the most hopeful, among the brightest and most beautiful stories you will ever hear. Some men falsely call it a sign of ill fortune, but in this world the ignorant say many things that aren't true. And the firmer they are in their view, the less likely it is that they're right. Remember that."

Brand spoke now with real passion, which was a thing he rarely did. Gil listened, and he recalled that Brand was one of the few men to have spoken with the immortal Halathrin in the last thousand years.

"Forget what you hear in the practice yard," Brand continued. "The Lost Huntress is one of the great heroes of the whole land of Alithoras. The constellation is named after her, and she is revered by the Halathrin. Indeed, she has another name. They call her also Arangar, which means noblebright. And you bear her sign on your very hands. It's no curse, but rather a blessing."

Gil felt suddenly special. He felt better. For some reason he felt that he could face down a thousand boys insulting him. He could look them in the eye with unflinching pride. Brand was good at doing that, good at giving people hope and dispelling the dark. But this once it was still not quite enough.

"But *why* do I bear the marks?"

Brand shook his head. "That, I don't know. It's a mystery, though legend says you're not the only prince of Cardoroth to have done so."

"No, that I've heard. But the other princes were born and died long ago. And it's not said that any of the royal line since Carnhaina herself have possessed magic." He paused. What he was about to say next was a secret that few knew, but Brand was one of them. In fact, he was his instructor in this as he was in so many other things. "Yet I do. Why am I different?"

Brand sighed. "I really don't know. But in no other time during the history of Cardoroth, since Carnhaina herself, has the kingdom been so threatened. I know nothing for certain, but I don't think you have the gift by accident. If you have it, you will have need of it. Fate works like that. At least in my experience."

Gil thought on that answer. He never spoke of the magic to anyone but Brand. None of the few who knew about it understood what it meant to possess it, but Brand did. He possessed it too. He taught him its uses just as he taught him many other things. The answer he had just been given felt right: if he possessed the power, he would have need of it.

Gil remembered something. "Is it true that you have met her ghost? The spirit of Carnhaina, I mean?"

There was a long pause. "Yes."

Brand removed a silver band from his finger, a signet ring, with a flat emerald set on top. Carved on the face of the stone was an image of a tower. Two diamonds, like the twin stars of the Lost Huntress, like the marks on Gil's palms, glinted above it.

Unexpectedly, Gil wanted to know something. "What was she like?"

"What was she like?" Brand folded his arms and closed his eyes. When he spoke, it was almost to himself.

"She was imperious. She was complex. She was powerful. Above all, she had a commanding presence. Her spirit only rose from death but briefly. It was a moment of great urgency, for the fate of the city hung in the balance. But when she spoke, I listened! Whatever else people say about her, she was a *queen*."

Gil thought about that. His grandfather had been something like that too. He wondered if one day people would ever listen to him, really listen. He had trouble imagining it.

Brand went on. "This was a lesson I learned from her. We are born into the world with nothing, and we leave with nothing. Nothing, except the name we make for ourselves. Thus are we remembered – so make your time count."

Brand sat back in his chair, and Gil considered what he had said. For some reason, it struck a chord with him. There was truth in that statement, hard-won truth. He stored the idea away to ponder sometime in the future.

He sensed that Brand had revealed all that he could, or would, about his heritage. It was not enough. He wanted to know *why* he had those marks. Was it just some random coincidence, or did it *mean* something? Did he possess magic for some specific purpose? But he would learn nothing more on those subjects now, so he brought the conversation back to where it had started.

"Why must I learn from the Swordmaster? Especially now? He'll hate me if you force him to do it. I practice with you every day at dawn, and you're better by far. Can't I just do that?"

Brand looked at him, as though assessing him.

"Gil. The Swordmaster *already* hates you. He hates you for who you are. But I don't send you there to learn swordcraft."

That was a surprise. The first part of the comment was brutally honest, but he appreciated that Brand always told him the truth. The second, he did not understand at all.

"But if I'm not going to the Swordmaster to learn what he teaches, then why am I going at all?"

"Because the other boys you train with are of the aristocracy, as are you. One day they'll be captains, generals, judges and the like. You'll spend your time as king dealing with those sorts of people. I send you there to get to know them, to understand them."

Gil thought about that. He saw immediately how much sense it made. It had nothing to do with swordcraft at all. He was about to ask why he also helped the stablemen to heap manure and look after the horses as one of his chores. But he did not. He saw for himself that he had been set that task to understand horses. That was critical for a king who might one day command an army, including cavalry regiments, in defense of the realm. Even more importantly, he would also gain an understanding of what it meant to be a common man or woman, what was important to them and what their worldview was. It was people like them who were the backbone of the realm.

Gil had a new insight into his training, and a deeper awareness of Brand's methods. He had much to think about.

Their discussion ended soon after. Messengers came to Brand, and the business of being regent cut short their time. Gil went away, his mind sifting through all that he had learned.

He passed once more through the tile-floored corridors of the palace. It was time to get something to eat, and though it was early the kitchens would be open, their preparations for dinner well underway.

He was not looking forward to tomorrow. The Swordmaster had expelled him, but Brand was going to disregard that. Sending Lornach to ensure there were no problems was sure to produce trouble of its own. Lornach was a commoner, but he had an attitude of supreme confidence that would set the Swordmaster's teeth on edge. There was going to be conflict there…

A voice came from behind him, startlingly close. "Why so deep in thought, young man? The troubles of the world aren't your own yet."

Gil looked around and smiled. It was Arell. She was said to be Brand's lover, but he had never seen any sign of it. But whatever the case, he liked her for she was beautiful and kind.

He opened his heart to her, and told her what had happened and what Brand had said.

"Listen to him," she advised when he was done. "Trust in Brand, and all he says. Men would follow him into the pit of hell."

Gil was a little taken aback. She was so certain in the way that she spoke.

"Why would anyone do that?" he asked.

Her response was swift. "Because he would do the same for them. Loyalty breeds loyalty," she said. Then she smiled and winked at him. "Remember that."

Her choice of words was no accident. She echoed one of Brand's sayings, the words he used to give special emphasis to something that would be of use throughout Gil's life.

He parted with Arell then, his mind a little clearer. Tomorrow would bring whatever it brought, but he would just face it and see what happened. And with Lornach going with him to see the Swordmaster, anything was possible.

Lornach was the Durlindrath, or at least one of them. There were two now. They jointly headed the royal bodyguards, the Durlin. One group guarded Brand, the other him. But Gil's group was bigger. Brand had been Durlindrath to the old king, and he did not need much in the way of guarding. No man in Cardoroth was his equal as a warrior. But if any came close, it was Lornach, and somehow Gil knew that when he met the Swordmaster tomorrow things would not go well.

He tried to put it all from his mind. It had been a long day, and he was hungry. He ate a quick meal, then went to his room. He was exhausted, and he pulled off his boots and got into bed in his clothes. No one would know.

Sleep came quickly. But just as quickly came the strange dream that had troubled him lately. He tossed and turned, rising up toward wakefulness, but then falling again into a deeper sleep. The dream gripped him this time and did not let go.

His body drifted through a dark place. The only light came from a sickly moon, yellow and blotched, partly concealed behind scudding clouds.

He slowed, and a forest grew about him. Trees stood tall and silent, as though watching. Their dark limbs reached forth beneath the fitful light, and shadows played across their leaves, making them seem like fingers that curled and clawed, always seeking.

Suddenly, he knew this place. It was in Cardoroth, but a part of countryside that few ever traveled. It was the pine

21

woods that surrounded Lake Alithorin, only hours from the city. Its reputation was grim.

Gil felt malice in the air. It was like a chill wind that blew right through him, yet nothing moved in the dark place except the shifting dance of yellowed light and forest shadows.

And then the trees seemed to arch, to form an aisle, and he saw beyond them into a dead-grassed glade, and wished that he had not.

His feet did not move. But he glided once again, ghost-like, and entered a world within a world. The grass below him was withered. The leaves of the surrounding trees hung limp, like dead fingers. The moon glared down now, free from its shroud of drifting clouds, peering like the watchful eye of a cruel cat, hunting, stalking, playing with a mouse caught in the open.

Gil shivered. In the center of the glade was a woman. Tall, thin, cloaked in shadow. Evil fell from her like leaves from a dead tree. Cold and hard was her swift glance, devoid of life, and her pale hand, pallid beneath the sickly moon, rose slowly but surely and pointed at him.

The woman spoke. Her voice welled as though from the earth itself, or an ancient tomb newly opened. But she did not address Gil. Rather, she chanted, and her hollow voice slowly filled the dark.

Murder and mayhem. Mayhem and murder. Seep from the ground. Rain from the sky. Float in the air all around. Malice and wrath, betrayal and treachery, bring the world woe and bring the world deviltry. Let the earth weep blood. Bring all to ruin. Crush hope and devour light.

Gil moaned. The woman paid him no heed. Her finger still pointing at him like a marker of doom, she turned her head and looked down. Beside her, Gil now saw, kneeled an acolyte. The man stood and took a step forward at some hidden command. In his hand he bore a curved knife. It glinted with dull moonlight.

Though the acolyte served the woman, there was terror in his eyes. That fear grew and spread. It gripped Gil. His breath caught in his chest, and he could not breathe. He tried to scream, but found no voice for his horror. And like a shadow that leaped and danced, it spread from the glade and filled the forest.

The forest trembled, and then the dark fear was out, out into the wide lands beyond, and Gil wondered if this was no mere dream but the casting of a spell.

The marks on his palms burned as though with fire, and suddenly a second lady stood in the glade. Tall she was, and a great spear she held in her jeweled fingers. One glimpse he caught of her, and then he woke.

Sweat drenched his pillow, and he lurched upright on his bed and gulped in the sweet night air. There he sat and trembled, waiting for his terror to subside.

2. The Tower of Halathgar

Dawn came after a long night, but Gil was already up. The dream hung over him like a cloud, stronger and darker than he had ever felt it before, but he tried to shrug it off.

Most mornings started in a particular way for him, and he liked the routine of it. The half hour before the sun came up was a time of peace. It was time that he spent with Brand, and it was the part of the day that he loved most and where his real training was conducted.

First, came the weapons practice. That was mostly with a sword, but Brand was introducing him to new things lately: daggers, staffs, spears and bare hand fighting.

This morning, it was a long sword that they used. Brand's was his own blade, the one he carried with him always, but Gil used a wooden training weapon, at least for sparring. For practicing techniques in the air, he used a real blade, sharp and dangerous.

The dawn air was still cool, and the sweat that soaked his tunic felt cold and clammy every time he rested. Where they practiced now, in an outside courtyard attached to the Durlin chapterhouse, a breeze blew through the lattice work and vines that blocked away the outside world. It made things even cooler, but the fresh air was vitalizing, and Gil inhaled deeply.

He slowed his breathing as Brand had taught him, using his abdomen rather than his chest. He felt relaxed as he sparred his teacher, moving sure-footed and purposefully. Without warning, he dropped low and swept his wooden blade at Brand's legs. It was a move the

Swordmaster had showed the boys, but it did not work on Brand. Quicker than Gil would have thought possible, the other man stepped forward and brought his blade down to stop suddenly above Gil's head. It would have been a killing stroke in a real battle, and Brand had executed it while Gil was still trying to perform his own technique, even though he had moved first.

Brand stepped back. "Don't use flashy moves, Gil. You left yourself unguarded there to perform it. No matter how good a move looks, always ask yourself how a skilled opponent would combat it. Add nothing to your repertoire until you fully understand its strengths and weaknesses."

Gil nodded. "I should have known better. I thought that surprise might have outweighed leaving myself open."

"Surprise is a factor in fighting, but not if it comes at too high a price. Anyway, that move isn't really intended for surprise. It does serve a function though."

"How should it be used, then?"

"It's for a man on foot fighting a mounted warrior. The target is the horse, rather than the rider. Dropping low gives you access to the horse's legs, and because of the rider's height, it takes you beneath his slashing blade. But it still must be timed just right, or you can get trampled or stabbed."

Gil suddenly saw how it would work that way, but he did not like it.

"It's a cruel thing to attack the horse instead of the rider."

Brand looked away. "So it is, but war is a cruel master. A man must sometimes do things that he would rather not, if he is to survive. What's the alternative?"

Gil had no answer for that. As was his way, Brand was teaching more than just swordcraft, no matter that they were in the middle of a sparring session. Always, he prepared him mentally for the things he practiced physically.

They continued to spar for a while longer. The sun rose slowly, and then Brand took him through a new technique. It was the same forward step and overhead blow that Brand had used earlier.

They went slowly at first, Gil standing a little behind and to the side so that he could copy the movements.

"Picture it in your mind first," Brand advised. "Whenever you practice the technique, see how the feet move, see how the sword is lifted – still held protectively in front of the body. Visualize it coming up, but not too high, and then imagine the footwork and arm movements coming together with a sudden hammering motion." Brand cut down in the final sequence of the technique, dropping his bodyweight to add force to the blow.

Gil tried it several times. It was not as easy as it looked.

"Keep on practicing, Gil. Imagine it first, and then execute it slowly. As with everything else I teach you, you'll gradually unify thought and action. Eventually, the two become one. The aim is to reach a point where the body acts by itself. It adjusts, and it does what's necessary without your conscious thought. When you can do that, then you're truly fast."

Gil wondered if he would ever reach that stage. It seemed beyond him, but so too had many things that he once doubted he would be able to do that were now second nature to him.

The sun was now fully risen, and the vines on the latticework cast dappled shadows across the paved floor of the courtyard.

"Time for another exercise," Brand announced. "Put away the sword."

Gil hung the wooden blade in one of the racks on the wall, and then he came back.

"Sit down, and face the sun," Brand instructed.

Gil sat cross-legged. Excitement built within him, for as much as he loved the way of the blade, he knew what was coming next and he loved it even more. It was for this, he felt, that he was born.

"Close your eyes," Brand continued.

Gil did so, and he attained a measure of peace and tranquility, though he knew as he progressed he would have to do the same thing with his eyes open. One day, he might have to do it under the stress of battle.

"Reach forth with your mind," Brand instructed. "Feel the light and warmth of the sun."

Hesitantly, Gil did so. He was still new at this, but the procedure was becoming familiar.

"Become one with it," Brand said. "Bring it into yourself ... and then focus on the palm of your hand. Let it out, transform it into fire."

Gil struggled at this point. He had no mastery of the magic yet, for all that he knew it was his passion in life. Sometimes it worked for him, and sometimes it did not.

But this time he felt it flutter to life. Flame leaped from his palm, and then it fluttered and dimmed only to flare again. It was unsteady, but it was there.

He opened one eye a slit and saw that Brand held a small ball of flame in his hand. It burned with a bright light, and neither flared nor dimmed. It was a constant thing, and Gil envied him that control.

"Lòhrengai is alive," Brand whispered. It was the true name of the magic; it was a name from the old tongue, from the immortal Halathrin themselves.

Brand passed the ball of flame from one hand to the other with casual ease.

"Lòhrengai is alive," he said. "The magic is all around us. We reach out and take it. We transform it, but it is alive. It's unpredictable. Perhaps it even has a will of its own. And even as we shape it, it works to shape us. Remember that."

Gil was having trouble concentrating. As sometimes happened when he used lòhrengai, his palms itched. Suddenly, he remembered the dream from the night before and he lost the ball of flame completely. It dimmed and then died out, and his hand felt cold and empty.

Brand twisted his hand and his own ball of flame dissipated into the air as though becoming mere sunlight again.

"I had a dream last night," Gil said. "Do you think that a dream can be a dream and yet be true at the same time?"

Brand did not answer at once. He cocked his head as though in thought, and then he shrugged.

"Not normally," he replied. "But you are not quite normal. The magic you possess and your heritage make it so."

Gil tried a slightly different approach. "Have you ever had a dream that turned out to be real?"

Brand looked at him solemnly. "No, I have not. But that doesn't mean anything."

"Why not?"

"Because I'm not you."

It was a simple answer. But as was Brand's way, he had said something as a simple fact that also had a deeper meaning, and Gil could follow his train of thought. Just because people were similar on the surface did not mean they were not profoundly different from each other.

"Well," he said. "I had a dream last night, and at the time it seemed as real as the two of us talking now."

"Tell me of it," Brand said. There was a note in his voice that Gil could not quite place. It might have been unease. Or perhaps not, for there was no sign of it in the other's eyes.

So Gil told him of the dream, and that last night was not the first time. It was a dream that he had been having for weeks. But it had somehow become more vivid, more real.

"And it was the first time that I saw the other woman," he added.

Brand looked thoughtful, which was far better than the attitude of dismissal Gil had feared. He should have known that Brand would take him seriously.

"Tell me more about the second woman."

Gil tried to remember the details. "She was large. She was dressed very well, and extremely regal. But she held a spear in her hand, which was rather strange, though she seemed like she knew how to use it. But she didn't. Instead, she watched and said nothing."

He paused, remembering more details. Which also was strange for a dream. Normally, they became vague rapidly, but this one seemed easy to recall.

"When I looked into her eyes," he continued, "the marks on my palms burned."

Brand seemed suddenly alert. If he had looked interested before, now his eyes glittered with an intelligent fierceness that he did not attempt to hide.

"What does it all mean?" Gil ventured.

"Nothing," Brand answered. "Or everything. Who can say with certainty? But the lady with spear, I think, was Carnhaina. She is quite distinctive, and her presence, or at least the presence of her ghost, makes me wonder what else of the dream may be true, and that whatever it portends will turn out to be of great significance."

Gil was not sure if he really believed any of that. Why should a long-dead queen appear in one of his dreams, even if they were related?

"What should we do?" he asked.

Brand turned to him after several moments of thought. "You've never been to the tomb of Carnhaina before, have you?"

"No," Gil said.

"Then we'll go there. And we'll do it tonight. It's part of your heritage anyway, and you should pay your respects."

Gil wondered what exactly Brand had in mind. No one visited tombs at night.

"Do you think she'll appear, as once she did for you?"

"No," Brand answered. "She has only ever appeared at times of great need. But we'll go there anyway."

Gil knew that Brand was worried, but it was not his way to show it. Nor was there any reason to suppose Cardoroth was in any great danger. He had only had a dream, after all. But not even his grandfather had ever taken him to Carnhaina's tomb before. He really did not know what to expect. Perhaps, in Brand's own words, everything or nothing.

Their practice for the day was over, and Gil went to the stables for rest of morning. It was not that far away, and he quickly found Brand's black stallion. The horse was old now, but he had sired many of the finest horses in Cardoroth. Gil and Brand were the only ones who ever rode him, but there was no time for that today.

"Hello, boy," Gil said, after letting himself in the stall and stroking the great horse's flanks.

30

The stallion snorted his own greeting, but as he moved Gil noticed something was not quite right. He took the horse by the halter, and got him to move around a little.

There it was. The shoe on his left rear leg seemed loose. Gil studied it a little more, and then fed him a ration of chaff and grain.

He left the stallion then, carefully closing the stall door behind him, and went in search of the farrier.

He found him in his work shed near the grain bins and equipment rooms. He was a tall man, normally quiet and grim, with black hair and a bristling black beard streaked with silver. Just at that moment he was shoeing a horse, quickly hammering in a nail while holding the horse's leg up at the same time.

Gil waited until the man was finished. "Good morning, master Fereck," he said.

The farrier nodded, but did not speak.

"Brand's black has a shoe coming loose, I think," Gil said into the silence.

The other man slipped his hammer through a loop in his trousers, and then he wiped his hands down his leather apron.

"I'll have a look and see this morning," he answered.

"Thank you, sir," Gil said. He followed Brand's example and showed respect to men such as this. The farrier, and the men like him that Gil knew, were men of skill and they deserved it. Not to mention, as Brand pointed out, the craftsmen who shoed horses, forged swords, constructed bows and the like did things upon which a warrior's life depended. It was wise to acknowledge that, and to stay in their good graces.

Gil turned to leave, but the farrier, for all that he seldom spoke much, was not done.

"One last thing," the man said.

Gil turned around, somewhat surprised.

"I know what you did," Fereck said.

"I beg your pardon?" Gil replied, confused.

"In the Swordmaster's practice yard, young man," the farrier explained. "I know what you did for the baker's daughter, and it was well done."

Gil blushed. "It was nothing, sir."

"It was more than nothing, and I for one will not forget."

The farrier turned away then, going about his business. He had said all that he was going to, but Gil felt a thrill run through him. The farrier was a quiet man, a reserved man, and praise from the likes of him was always understated and rare. That made it special to hear.

Gil went away, feeling on top of the world. As he walked, a realization came to him. The aristocracy tended to stick together, but so too did workers and tradesmen. Word had traveled fast of yesterday's events, and he did not doubt that many now knew the story, and he had gained some friends he had not had before. It was a good feeling.

Brand, of course, must have foreseen that he would learn lessons like that, and that he would gain a better understanding of such people, of human nature itself. It was why he had been asked to deal with them in the first place, but he found that he liked them too. They were in many ways more real, more down to earth, more honest and just plain likeable compared to the run-of-the-mill aristocracy.

Gil spent some time in the palace library after that. He had been given a schedule of history books to read, mostly the memoirs of kings. They could, at times, be fascinating reading. So it was now, and before he knew it the afternoon had arrived and it was time to set aside a treatise on a centuries-old battle and head toward the Swordmaster's practice yard a little way into the city.

There was no sign of Lornach. But the Durlindrath was a busy man, and perhaps he was not free to come. If so, Gil was going to have trouble explaining his presence when he got to training. He had been expelled, and he had no business being there. Still, he did not think Lornach would let him down. He would be there, and his presence, though very much wanted, was also very likely to cause trouble. Gil could not guess how things were going to go between him and the Swordmaster.

When Gil arrived, the other boys were already there. They were practicing in pairs, and he felt their looks on him and heard the whisper of "nightborn" from some.

He passed down their line, and the looks and whispers ceased. But when he came to the baker's daughter, she stopped what she was doing and spoke to him.

"Hello, Gil."

He nodded and smiled, even if it was nervously. "Hello, Elrika."

He had no further chance to talk to her. The Swordmaster had seen him, and he had removed himself quickly from his seat and was in the process of striding over.

"How dare you—" he began, but that was as far as he got. Lornach was suddenly there. Where exactly he had come from, Gil did not know, but he was relieved.

He turned to look, and noticed that Brand's friend was not wearing the white surcoat of the Durlin, which signified his office. Instead, his clothes were plain.

"That's enough," Lornach said.

33

"And who the blazes are you?"

Lornach did not answer that. Instead, he delivered a message.

"I bear word from the regent," he said. "You're dismissed from your post. Another Swordmaster will take your place. Today."

The Swordmaster looked incredulous. Then he stood tall, towering above the much shorter man.

"The *regent* does not have that right. I was appointed by the king himself."

"No," Lornach said matter-of-factly. "Your *father* was appointed by the king. You weren't. The title of Swordmaster is honorary, and you have never been honored with it. You have no business here, and you are dismissed."

There were noises of shock from the line of students. The two men ignored that, and stared at each other.

"I'm the best swordsman in Cardoroth," the Swordmaster said. "No one can take my place. Who would even dare?"

Lornach seemed amused. "You're not the best swordsman in Cardoroth. You're a pompous ass. You have no skill with the blade. At all. And that makes you unfit for the job, besides never being appointed to it."

"How dare you!"

"I dare, because Brand has made me the Swordmaster. Now, once more, you are dismissed."

"You can't dismiss me!"

Lornach shook his head slowly. "I just did."

The baron drew his weapon. "This is an insult," he said through clenched teeth. "I will not permit it. Draw your blade, peasant. I will show you a real Swordmaster."

Lornach looked intently at the other man. His expression was no longer amused. It was cold, cold as ice, and Gil felt fear grip him. The Swordmaster had gone too far in drawing his weapon.

"I would not injure you," Lornach said clearly. "But if you don't sheathe your blade, I'll not guarantee your safety."

The face of the Swordmaster was red, and when he spoke he almost spat the words.

"Enough talk, peasant. Tell me your name, and nothing else. I would know that before I kill you."

Lornach sighed. "I'm generally known as Shorty, at least by my friends."

"An apt name. Now draw, or I'll spill your blood where you stand."

"We don't have to duel," Lornach said. "Accept the regent's decision, and move on with your life."

"This isn't a duel. Only the nobility duel against each other. You will never be that, no matter how you serve the regent, who is only a peasant himself. Now draw!"

Lornach's expression hardened, and the blade of his sword slid from its sheath with a quick rasp. Nevertheless, he did not look like a man ready to fight. If anything, he looked supremely bored.

Gil felt someone shuffle close behind him, and heard a whisper in his ear.

"Your friend is a dead man."

It was Turlak, the ringleader of the boys. Gil had heard that he was the son of a duke, but they had seldom spoken. He did not take his eyes off the scene before him, but whispered back.

"You don't know who he is, do you?"

"I know a dead man when I see one."

Gil grinned tightly. "He said his name was Shorty. But most in the city know him better as Lornach. You *have* heard of the king's champion and one of the great heroes of the war, haven't you?"

The older boy did not answer that. He had not known, for he and his father did not come to court and had not seen Brand's entourage.

Gil paid the boys gathered behind him no more heed. The Swordmaster had stepped into the open and assumed a long fighting stance. It was not one he had ever taught his students. Not Gil, anyway.

Lornach still seemed casual, and his sword wove tight but lazy circles in the air before him.

Suddenly the Swordmaster lunged. It was fast, faster than Gil had ever seen him move, but Lornach must have seen it coming. He stepped nimbly away to the side and did not even use his blade to deflect the other's.

Lornach grinned. "Really? No one taught you to keep the shoulder of your sword arm still so you don't signal your intention to strike? That's a basic error."

The Swordmaster went white. There was death in his eyes, but Lornach merely laughed.

Three more times the Swordmaster struck. Each effort failed, but for each of these attacks Lornach flicked out his sword, deliberately striking the other's body with only the flat of his blade and then dancing out of range.

The Swordmaster had become enraged. His face was twisted and his hands trembled. He tried his best to kill Lornach, but the king's champion was more than his match. When he was ready, Shorty casually disarmed his opponent with a short flick of his blade, a move that Gil had never seen, and the Swordmaster's weapon flew through the air.

The Swordmaster leaped to regain it, but Lornach was quicker, the point of his sword flashing to stop an inch from the other's neck. They both froze where they were, one crouching and reaching toward a blade, the other poised. They both knew that one wrong move would end in death, and it would not be Lornach's.

"I would leave now, if I were you," Lornach said. "Retrieve your sword some other time."

With great care, the Swordmaster straightened and stepped back. He shook violently, and cold fear was etched on his face.

"You are dismissed," Lornach said softly.

The Swordmaster left, but he drew himself together enough to manage a parting shot at Gil.

"I hold you responsible for this!" he hissed. "But your time will come. Think on this, meanwhile. Brand is regent. But he will usurp the throne. You will never be king. *Remember that!*"

Gil did not answer. He looked over at Lornach instead, but if the Durlindrath had paid any attention to what was said, he gave no sign.

Lornach, not even a little out of breath, addressed the students.

"Class is dismissed for the day. You may return tomorrow at the same time. But think on the two lessons you have just learned. Never underestimate an opponent. Never. No matter what they look like. And talk is cheap. If you wish to become accomplished, in any field, take these lessons to heart. The sweat of practice is worth more than empty words. Class dismissed."

The boys trailed away, beginning to talk among themselves as they left. Some cast dark looks at Gil, but Elrika smiled at him.

When they were gone, Lornach spoke. "Forget what the baron said. Brand will see you king. He'll not usurp your throne."

Obviously, he *had* heard the Swordmaster's words. But no more was said after that, even though Gil sensed that Lornach wanted to add more.

It was not the first time Gil had heard the Swordmaster's claim. He shrugged it off though. He did not believe it, but still, human nature being what it was, he was forced to accept the possibility. In a way, it did not matter. He had no wish to be king, no wish for all the responsibilities. He had seen what that had done to his grandfather. He did not want that. Not at all. What he wanted was to keep learning lòhrengai. That was his true passion. With that knowledge, with the gift that was in him, he could make the world a better place.

But no one ever accepted that. He would be king, they said. He half wished that Brand *would* usurp the throne, but that would be a breach of trust, and just the thought of that possibility, of an action like that from a man such as Brand that he admired so much, struck Gil like a blow.

It was a quiet walk back to the palace with Lornach, for they both seemed to be occupied with private thoughts.

They said their goodbyes once they were within the ancestral home of the kings of Cardoroth. And now, Gil realized, Brand's home. Much had happened, and Gil needed to think. Not to mention that at some time during the night he would be going to Carnhaina's tomb. That would undoubtedly be a sobering experience.

Much seemed to be happening these days, and Gil wished he could talk things over with his mother. But she was not there, and he did not really know when she was coming back. She had said she would be with his grandparents, and that was not hard to believe. She was as close to them as she was to her own parents, but Gil had a feeling there was more going on. It was almost as if he had been left in the care of Brand for some other reason. He felt slightly abandoned, but then he dismissed that thought. It was not true, and whatever his mother had done she had done for good reason. And her trust in Brand was just as deep as that of his grandfather's.

The rest of the afternoon passed, and the evening drew on to night. Gil slept, but he woke instantly when he heard a soft knock on his door. He got out of bed, already dressed and in his boots, and opened the door. It was Brand, come to take him to Carnhaina's tomb, but strangely there was no one else with him.

Brand must have sensed exactly what he was thinking. "We go alone, for this," he said.

They spoke little after that. Like dark wraiths they slipped out of the palace. There were no bodyguards. There were no palace staff. There was no one save him and Brand.

Out through the gardens they went, and into the city beyond. It was late, near the midnight hour, and the streets were quiet. They saw few abroad, and those they did see were revelers well-steeped in drink, or the furtive cutthroats who lurked in the dark to prey upon them.

Neither was a problem for Brand. He ignored the first, and the second he seemed to spy out with an uncanny prescience that amazed Gil. He would slow, place a hand on the hilt of his sword and stare into the hidden shadows until whoever hid there knew their ambush would fail and scuttled away.

Brand's eyes were bright, almost eager for battle, and the hunters who hid must have sensed that in his every move and glance. There were easier targets, and they did not long survive on the streets themselves unless their instincts told them when to fight and when to run.

They went through a park. There was no light except for the stars above, and cold fear settled over Gil. This was no place to be at night. Yet Brand walked with sure purpose, his gaze searching the shadows and his strides relaxed and easy.

Before Gil knew it they had come to a cobbled street again, and there before them was the Tower of Halathgar. It reached up into the night, bordered by the park and the trees that grew there. There was light here, some cast by fitful street lamps and some that spilled out of the structure's lower windows.

Gil looked up. Only the base of the tower was lit. Higher, it disappeared into shadows, and somewhere within was the fabled sanctum of Queen Carnhaina. Here, legend held, she came to study the stars away from the palace lights and to work magic while the city slept. Looking at the dark tower now, wreathed in night-shadows, a silhouette of tightknit stone blocks that thrust from the earth like an arm reaching up from the grave, he believed it.

They came to the door at the base of the tower. Two guards stood there, wearing the livery of soldiers of Cardoroth. They did not seem surprised to see someone, least of all the regent and the heir to the throne, and Gil surmised that they knew of this visit.

Brand greeted them, and they saluted him. Quickly, the door was opened and Brand led Gil through. One of the soldiers passed the regent a burning torch, and then the door was closed again.

Gil stood behind Brand while they waited for their eyes to adjust. His heart raced, but Brand seemed as calm as ever. There were signs of a trapdoor on the floor, and beyond that the beginning of a spiral staircase that wound toward the top.

Brand paused, as though in momentary doubt, but Gil caught a glimpse of his face in the ruddy light and saw that his eyes were far away. He was remembering something.

With the slightest of shrugs, Brand started up the stairs.

Gil was confused. Surely that was the wrong way, and they should be opening the trapdoor to go down into the basement.

"I thought we were going to her tomb?" he asked, and even his whispered voice seemed unnatural and loud in the quiet.

"We are," Brand answered. "But it's not in the basement as men think. Instead, it's atop the pinnacle of the tower. You'll see."

Brand did not pause. He walked up the stairs, sure of his way as always, and Gil envied him his confidence.

The stairwell circled the inside of the tower wall and they passed a series of doors that led to inner rooms. They reached the ninth level, and there they found another two guards. No one spoke, but they exchanged nods, and Gil felt the eyes of the soldiers on him, weighing him up.

They came soon to a door that opened onto the top of the tower. It was closed, but apparently not locked, and Brand opened it with a soft touch of his hand. The ancient hinges made no noise.

Brand stepped through first, and he rested his torch against the wall. When Gil stepped through, the regent closed the door behind them.

Gil looked around. He saw an open platform and above the great vault of the sky, star-laden and vast.

Brand led him forward, stepping on soft feet, and Gil followed closely. A chill wind blew into their faces. The city stretched out below. It lay beneath a blanket of shadows, but lights twinkled here and there within it, and the torchlit main streets wound through the dark like rivers of fire.

In the center of the platform a stone monument rose knee-high from the floor. Brand, without hesitation, moved toward it. The structure's sides were slabs of red marble, engraved with strange script and sculpted with scenes of battle. Carved carrion crows, their wings cut sharp-edged and lifelike into the stone, circled above battling armies while wolves prowled the horizon. The single slab that served as a top was tightly fitted to the four sides, but there were groves in the stone as though once it had been removed without care. And black stains, perhaps scorch marks, covered it.

Gil felt a sudden chill beyond even the breeze that blew across the high pinnacle of the tower.

"We should not have come here. Not at night."

Brand turned his gaze upon him, and his eyes were bright.

"I'm too busy during the day."

Gil did not quite believe that. He thought Brand was holding back. However open he seemed to be, he *did* have secrets. Then the words of the Swordmaster rose sinuously in his mind. This, the Swordmaster had said, was the man who would usurp his throne. And he was alone with him in the tower of a long-dead queen. Alone, and no one knew where they were except a handful of guards, and those guards were loyal to Brand.

Gil dismissed such thoughts. They were unworthy. Brand was a great man, a hero, and trusted by all. Instead, he concentrated on the slab that formed the top of the structure. An image of Carnhaina was on it. He was sure it was the same woman from his dreams. She was unmistakable.

He thought back over the long history of the city. It was old. Near a thousand years had passed since its founding, and Carnhaina was there close to its beginning. It was she who had defended it from the hordes that had come from the north. She had beaten them, as she had also beaten the hordes that came from the south. Each had been led by mighty sorcerers of antiquity, but she had defeated them all. But why was she so forgotten? Little was known of her, except that she was also named the witch-queen. Was she a hero or a villain?

A sudden noise broke his thoughts. There was movement too. He looked out over the pinnacle of the tower and into the park. There, he saw the tops of the trees. They seemed very close, and they swayed in the breeze. But something moved among their branches.

Gil strained, searching the darkness. There were crows there. Something had disturbed their roosting and they flapped and hopped from branch to branch. He heard also their rasping call, a croak that sounded oddly human, as though there were words in it. But there were not.

The breeze picked up, and then went still unexpectedly. The crows seemed to go mad, flapping and cawing and some even took to wing in the shadowy air.

Above, the stars twinkled bright. Halathgar was there above the tower, the two stars shining bright against the black sky, looking down like eyes.

The marks on Gil's palms itched. And then they seemed to burn like fire. He held them up, but they looked as they always did.

Brand was not still. He stepped back, back toward the door. In one hand the cold steel of his sword glimmered. In the other, he held once more the torch.

The regent came forward, slowly. The crows cawed and flapped as the light flared and sputtered. The branches of the trees creaked, and the great trunks groaned as the breeze stirred to life again. It came and went according to some rhythm beyond Gil's guess or understanding.

And then, suddenly, everything went still again. The trees did not move. The wind did not blow. In the branches, the now-silent crows merely watched the tower with beady eyes.

Gil's palms burned all the more.

3. Four Horsemen Shall Come

Gil stood perfectly still. Something was happening, but he did not know what. He glanced at Brand, but the regent did not move either, and there was an expression on his face that Gil had never seen before. It might have been awe. It might have been fear. He could not tell which, but that he had never seen it before was unsettling.

The dust on the flagstones of the tower floor rose and seethed. More than that, the top of the monument rattled, and dust sprayed out from its edges. Light glimmered, over and above the fitful flicker of Brand's torch, but it seemed to have no source unless it was the stirring dust itself.

And that dust began to take shape. An ethereal form rose from it in a swirl of color, and Gil staggered back. Brand did not move.

Gil had thought the slab was a monument. Now, he understood that it was a sarcophagus. The image of a woman, tall and majestic, solidified from the dust. She gazed down at the man and the boy, her eyes terrible and stern. They were blue, cold as Lake Alithorin in winter, but her skin was pale, and her unbound hair shone like spilled blood. Luxurious curls ran down her back and shimmered in the shadowy air. She was a massive figure, heavy-boned and thick-limbed. A gold torc gleamed brilliantly about her neck, and her body was clad in a tunic of many colors. In her right hand she grasped an iron-headed spear as though ready to strike.

Her stare bored into them. "Who comes hither? Who disturbs my rest?"

They did not answer. The eyes of the long-dead queen burned upon Brand, and there was recognition in them.

"You," she said, pointing at him with her spear. "You I know. Brand you are called, though other names you might yet earn. If you live."

Her chill gaze fell on Gil. His blood turned to ice, but his hands felt like they were on fire.

She studied him long before she spoke. "You also I know, blood of my blood, heir to my realm. You I know, though you do not yet know yourself."

She paused. The breeze blew across the top of the tower, and her hair ruffled and moved. But Gil could see through her, see that she was at once real, and not real. It made his heart thud in his chest, but the blood in his body seemed frozen in place.

"Do you know who I am?" she said to Gil, her spear poised, but her glance sharper still. "Speak!"

Gil found his voice. "You are Carnhaina. Once you ruled this realm. Once, you were Queen of Cardoroth."

His voice failed him after that. But she did not seem to notice.

"Yes, that was me." She spoke almost as though she were talking of someone else. "And you are Gilcarist. Heir to my throne." She paused again. "You are younger even than I thought."

She glanced thoughtfully at Brand. "There is danger abroad," she said.

Brand held her gaze. "When is there not?"

She laughed at that. The crows in the trees flapped madly.

"Well spoken!" she replied. "You will be ready, but being ready is not enough. Not this time." She seemed as though she would say more on the subject, but then she broke the regent's gaze momentarily before looking back and saying something obviously different from what she had intended. "Is the boy ready?"

Brand shrugged. "Ready for what? But I have brought him here, so you can ask him yourself."

"Then I shall!"

She looked at Gil, and he felt the weight of her mind upon him. He wondered how Brand dared speak to her as he did.

"Well, boy. Are you ready? Are you ready to learn who you are?" Her gaze scrutinized him, measured him, found out all his innermost secrets. "Are you ready to learn what you most desire? To know why your palms are marked? To know your destiny?"

Gil nodded. His voice was a whisper. "Yes."

"And if you do not like what you discover?" she pressed him.

He did not know what to say, and the fear that he felt irked him, so he followed Brand's nonchalant example and shrugged.

"Why don't you tell me, and then we'll both know."

She stared at him a moment. Starlight glinted on the tip of her spear, and it seemed as though the whole night held its breath. But then, with a backward toss of her head, she roared with laughter.

After a moment she fixed him with her glinting gaze. "I guess you're as ready as you can be. Brand has taught you well, and your blood shows."

The once-queen of Cardoroth stood silent a moment. The night was still. The crows were subdued, and the starlit heavens twinkled and shone amid the great dark.

"It will be dangerous," she said, her voice now turning soft and solemn. "Learning who you are, and more importantly who you can be, will not be safe. Do you accept that danger?"

47

Gil looked into her eyes. "I do," he answered boldly.

"You would know the meaning of the marks on your palms?" she challenged.

"I would."

"You may not like what you discover."

"So be it," he answered.

The spirit that was Carnhaina drew herself up. "Then look and learn!"

She swept up the arm that carried her spear, and the air shimmered. When it stilled, Gil looked no longer upon reality but a vision. His eyes fixed upon it, drawn as if by a will beyond his own.

He saw the tallest mountains of the land, the far northern borders of Alithoras. They were cold, and the great stretches of pine forests that clad them were draped with snow. Ice covered the ridges. Yet there was peace there, a sense of tranquility. And cold though it was, the sky was blue and the sun shone down benevolently.

Gil sensed Brand stir beside him. Then the vision flickered. Swift images came of a lake that might have been Lake Alithorin. Then there were cities and realms and wild lands of hill and forest. There were battles. Battles with men and creatures that were not men. There was sorcery and magic, and a great sweep of time and distance. There were castles and farms and endless leagues of long grass, and then the vision cleared and stilled once more.

Now, the land was dry and desolate. The hot sun hammered down. The sand and dirt shimmered. Gil felt a sense of malice, a threat of ill-will in the very air. This was Grothanon, the land of the ancient enemy, the land that threatened all of Alithoras, and there was a presence there. Gil concentrated on that, focused his mind upon the source of that hatred. But even as he did so Carnhaina quickly swept her hand down and the vision ceased.

The witch-queen gazed at him, and there was something unreadable in her eyes. Gil had the feeling that she had intended to show more, but had stopped sooner than she planned.

"Alithoras!" she said, her voice ringing. "Our land. A great land, but there is evil within it. And only by the deeds of heroes is that evil kept at bay."

She leaned upon her spear, and turned her gaze upon Brand.

"You," she continued. "You have fought in that battle, and have a sense of what threatens the land. But you sit on a chair as a play-king, not upon the throne of Cardoroth. But if you wished it, you could take the throne itself. None would stand in your way. You have proven yourself worthy, and the land *needs* you. Think, man, of the power you could wield. Why have you not taken it?"

Gil could not believe what he was hearing. This was his own great-grandmother, many times removed. Was she suggesting Brand usurp the throne of her own descendant?

Brand did not move. Still as a carven stone he stood, but he answered her.

"In truth," he replied, "I have considered it. I know exactly how to become king of Cardoroth, and I could do it in less than a week, if I so chose. But I have no interest in that."

Carnhaina gazed at him, then spoke. "You would be a great king. Perhaps even the greatest who ever ruled in Alithoras. Think on that, Brand of the Duthenor."

Her spear swept up again. Suddenly an image of Brand stood there, gazing back at himself. This Brand was older, but not yet old. A mighty crown rested on his head, and liegemen knelt before him. Behind, misted and swirling, were other cities and other lands. This Brand ruled them all, and his glance was piercing as a sword. Wisdom was in it, and great joy and sorrow. It was Brand, and not Brand.

The regent laughed. "You seek to test me, Carnhaina, but you know what I want, and it isn't that. My goal is far less lofty, and even so I guess now that I will never achieve it. Not directly anyway. My destiny, if there is such a thing, is different. And I accept that."

"Destiny," whispered the queen. "Destiny is what you make it, and I know you perceive that. Still, I will not say that your answer is wrong."

Gil had a feeling that they were taking about things of which they both understood, but he knew none of it. Though it did occur to him that Brand would be a great king, better than he would, and that if the regent usurped the throne it would relieve him of the responsibility himself. He had, in truth, no desire to rule. He wanted to learn more of the magic. Lòhrengai was his love, and with that he could make the world a better pace.

But he had no time to think now. The gaze of the queen fell upon him, and it was as though she read his every thought. She was a spirit creature, dead long centuries, but who knew what powers she had in life, and retained still in death? He trembled under her scrutiny, but did not back away though his every instinct was to turn and run.

"And you?" she said. "What of your destiny? Would you know it?"

"Yes," Gil answered, and it seemed that the air in his throat had turned to ice.

"Then," the queen replied, "behold!"

Up swept the spear again, and it pointed straight at him. He could not blink. He could not look away. And suddenly he wished that he had indeed fled, but his feet were rooted to the spot just as his eyes could not turn away.

50

He saw himself. He was in the forest surrounding Lake Alithorin again. The trees were dark and shadowy about him. At his feet lay Brand. Dead. Blood covered the regent. Blood from some mighty battle, some struggle that not even the great Brand could survive. His eyes, lifeless, stared up at the sky. The vision swept away, and the marks on Gil's palms burned and ached.

He looked up at the witch-queen, confused but defiant. "That tells me nothing. Tell me why I have these marks!" He lifted up his hands and white light glimmered about them. "Why? And why show me such visions? Brand can't be both dead and king in the future. Tell me the truth!"

Carnhaina gazed at him steadily. Her face was a mask, hiding any trace of what she felt. Just like Brand, Gil thought.

The witch-queen answered, and her voice was softer than it had been.

"The truth is that destiny must be discovered. Or made. Made from the day-to-day events that shape your life. Made from the choices that you make. Both visions are true. Both are false. And I can explain it no clearer than that. But you will understand when you are there, when you are faced with choices. For now, know that the marks serve a purpose. Through them, you shall find yourself."

Gil knew when someone was hiding the truth from him. Not lying, but not revealing all that they knew.

"Those are just words," he said. "They mean nothing."

Carnhaina fixed him with her glittering eyes. "Words, is it? You will learn that no force of arms, no power of magic, no strength of will is as great as words. One day, you will know that. But in the meantime, I give you this. Pay heed, for the eyes of the dead see what is to come, or what has already passed. Pay heed, for this shall shape your life. And Brand's."

Carnhaina straightened. Midnight shadows darkened her hair, but the light of stars was in her eyes and she looked fierce, regal, deadly. Deadly and more dangerous than any person Gil had ever met.

"Four horsemen shall come," she said. "And that you shall know them, these are their names. First, Death. Next War. Then shall follow Time. Last, and greatest of them all, Betrayal."

The dead queen lifted up her spear as though it were a scepter of authority.

"Beware! For things are not always as they seem. Before the sun sets tomorrow you shall see Death. It shall mark a beginning, for from thence forward a hidden assassin will try to kill you. He may or may not succeed. But success or failure is still victory for him."

Gil did not understand the queen's words. How could a horseman be called Death? How could a failure be success? It made no sense, but he felt nonetheless a chill run through him, and he saw that Brand looked at the queen intently.

"Discover the identity of the assassin. You will have friends to help you. When you know, the truth shall protect you."

Carnhaina turned to Brand. "You have seen your death," she said. "In the dark forest around Lake Alithorin it shall come to pass. The boy will witness it."

"So be it," Brand answered. There was no trace of emotion in his voice. "No man lives forever."

Carnhaina leaned once more upon her spear, but the intensity of her eyes did not diminish.

"In truth," she said, "you are a fitting heir to me. You are a warrior and a lòhren – a user of magic. You could take the throne and live. It is yours, if you want it."

Brand shrugged. "I know temptation when I hear it. I also know that Cardoroth's army is my friend," he paused. "The aristocrats are irrelevant."

The queen laughed. A cold laugh, without mirth. "They always were. So, take the throne!" she urged. "Take it!"

Brand shook his head. "No. I don't want it. And even if I did, I still wouldn't take it."

Carnhaina studied him, and there was some emotion on her face that Gil could not decipher.

"Then," the queen said at length. "Know this. If you do not, the vision I showed shall come to pass. You will perish within the forests of Lake Alithorin."

Brand, as ever, showed no reaction. But he stood very still.

"As I say, all men die."

Gil thought the regent's voice was cold as the void, but notwithstanding that Brand showed nothing of what he felt, Gil still sensed the hot emotion that lay somewhere beyond sight.

Carnhaina laughed, and Gil suddenly wondered if she was sane.

"So be it," she answered, and she bowed her head.

Gil realized that she had begun to fade. She had seemed so present, but now there was no mistaking that she was a shade, an echo of someone who once had lived.

She lifted her head briefly toward Gil. "Remember the Mark of Halathgar," she said. "When you need help the most, call upon it …"

It was yet another puzzle to Gil. She was the queen of enigmas, and he sensed that although much was said that he did not understand, many things were the opposite of what they seemed. He felt that strikingly as her gaze rested on him. There was the promise of answers in that glance, and a hint that despite what she had urged Brand to do, she was really looking out for Gil, and for Cardoroth, in a way that made no sense now but would later.

Suddenly, the breeze gusted. Brand's torch guttered. When it flared to life once more, the spirit of Carnhaina was gone.

4. I am Death

Brand led Gil down the tower stairs in silence. If the guards had heard anything, they gave no sign. Nor did they speak. They looked ahead as though no one was there, and Gil did not blame them.

Out on the dark streets, Brand remained quiet. He was a man deep in thought, his face shadowed and his head bowed. He did not look like he wished to talk, but Gil risked a question.

"The stories of Carnhaina, the few that I've ever heard, are all strange. She proved that tonight. But what I want to know is … well, is she good or bad?"

Brand gave thought to that question before he answered. His pace did not slow, but his head came up a little and he cast a sideways glance at Gil.

"She was one who delved into sorcery," Brand said. "In truth, there is little difference between magic and sorcery, between what we call lòhrengai and what they call elùgai. Yet, I'm told that though she delved into elùgai, she did not go deeply down that path. The difference is not in the power itself, but in the use to which that power is put."

Brand slowed a little now. He looked over at Gil, assessing how much he understood of this.

"In short, the line between a lòhren and an elùgroth, an adept in dark sorcery, is finer than most think. But know this. It's far more important than labels. Often, we forget what people say, but we never forget how they make us feel. Remember that. And think on how Carnhaina made you *feel*. That will answer your question."

Gil considered that. Carnhaina certainly scared him, but she had treated him like an adult, too. Only Brand really did that. So, how did she make him feel? On reflection, he realized that in talking to her that he felt a part of something, a part of something great, a part of a long history of defiance against the evil in the world. And thinking of her last glance toward him, he sensed love there, and concern. No matter that she did not say it directly, *it was still there*. That was what he felt. He had learned another of Brand's lessons, and it was one of the best.

They spoke no further after that. Each had much to think about, and no one troubled them on the streets. It was late when they came back to the palace, and the guards admitted them into the building without comment.

Gil went to bed and fell swiftly asleep, but it was a troubled slumber and frequently his mind, drifting between waking and oblivion, pondered all of Carnhaina's words. But though he turned them over and over in his mind, he made little sense of them.

Eventually, he fell into a deeper sleep and straightaway he dreamed once again of the woman in the woods. It was the same as always, and yet somehow different too. This time, it went further.

The woman placed her bony hands on the acolyte. Whether to calm him or hold him against his will, Gil did not know. But the acolyte, though filled with terror, did not move. Still as a statue he stood, his face pale and his bulging eyes white in the moonlight, while the woman lifted her sickle shaped knife.

That part of Gil's mind that was aware even in the midst of a dream recoiled. It sought out the aid of Carnhaina who had in some way saved him from seeing this last time, but she was not there. Yet, on thinking of her, he found strength of his own and drew back to wakefulness.

He woke with a start, the dream shadowing him as though real and reluctant to let him escape, even when his eyes were open. Eventually, though, that feeling faded.

He fell asleep again after that, and was not troubled any further. Yet it seemed that he had only just fallen asleep when he woke once more. Time must have passed though, for light streamed in from the windows.

His first thought was that he was late for his early morning training with Brand, but he did not think that would be an issue. Not after last night. Brand would have slept in too. His second thought was that something was wrong.

He got up and dressed quickly. There was much noise out in the city streets while he did so. He heard it dimly even in the palace, and there were many passing feet out in the corridors, many more than usual even for this later hour of the morning. Worse, he heard muffled conversations as people hurried past his door, but one word was repeated and he heard it quite clearly. *Devil.*

When he was ready he opened the door and went out into the corridor. No one was here just now, not even the Durlin who usually guarded it at night.

He walked along a little further, and after a few turns and twists there were suddenly people everywhere. They looked frightened, and when they saw him they scattered. They knew what was happening, but had no wish to tell him for some reason.

Gil made up his mind. He would go to the throne room and talk to Brand. He would get the truth that way, and he knew Brand would be there. That was where the city leaders gathered in times of trouble, and Gil had a sense that trouble had come.

As he moved through the passageways they became increasingly busy. People were everywhere, standing and talking, and soldiers and messengers filled the gaps.

Gil was not sure what to do, for the way through seemed blocked, and he became increasingly alarmed at hearing the word *devil* repeated in low whispers. Something terrible was happening, and he could not get through to see Brand.

He was about to try to push his way ahead when suddenly he came face to face with Elrika, the last person he had expected to see. He saw her seldom even though her father was the palace baker, but hers was a friendly face so he greeted her and asked if she knew what was happening.

"I think so," she said, but she got no further. A group of soldiers pressed through and separated them, heading toward the throne room.

Elrika reached out for him and took him by the arm. "Follow me. We'll get separated if we're not careful."

She led him back the way he had come, but the press of people was growing and it was now almost as hard to go back as forward.

"Have you had breakfast yet?" she asked.

Gil shook his head. "No."

"Then we'll head to the kitchen."

Gil wanted to ask her to explain what was happening, but the kitchen was not far away and they could talk properly there without the noise and racket that filled the corridors.

They passed along a few more passageways, and then Elrika turned down a corridor that was much quieter. At its end was a stairwell. This they followed for several flights until they came out again in a passageway Gil was more familiar with. Before them was a set of oak doors, old and worn, and though he was not sure if he had ever been through them before he knew they were at the back of the kitchen, the entry the servants used.

Elrika went through. The doors swung closed behind them, and straightaway the noise died down. There were people here, working away at chopping vegetables and dicing meat. They gave Elrika a quick glance and then paid her no more heed. They had seen her many times before and if Gil was with her, then he was nothing to worry about either. They did not seem to recognize him, and he liked that.

They passed through several other rooms, one of which contained a long bank of hearths with great brick chimneys, but there were few fires lit this morning. At lunch and dinner there would be more.

Gil had been here before, but he had been much younger. He barely remembered any of it, but Elrika knew where she was going and she quickly turned into a side room. This was the bakery, and hundreds of loaves of still-warm bread cooled on wooden racks along with many varieties of pastries.

Elrika reached out and grabbed one of the pastries and then sat down at a small table in the corner.

"Hungry?" she asked.

"Starving," Gil answered.

She carefully tore the pastry in half, and gave him one of the portions. It was filled with a combination of savory meats and dried fruits.

She took a bite of hers. "My favorite," she said.

Gil tried his piece. He had never had it before, and he found it delicious.

She took another bite and then leaned forward over the table toward him.

"This is what I know," she said. "My father heard it direct from the first messenger this morning who came in from the West Gate." She paused to take another bite of the pastry.

"The Arach Neben," she said, using the old name for the gate, "is closest to the dark forests that surround Lake Alithorin. The messenger said that a devil had come from there, a devil such as Cardoroth has never seen before."

There were many legends about those woods, and Gil had heard plenty of them. Dark things were said to dwell there, and he believed it, though he had never seen any himself. The forest was out of bounds to him.

"What did the messenger mean by the word devil, though? Some sort of creature?"

Elrika shook her head at once. "No. Not a creature. A man, or something like a man. And he rides upon a horse."

Gil went perfectly still, and his stomach churned with sudden fear. He remembered back to last night. It had seemed like a dream in the light of day, but he knew it was not. What had Carnhaina said? He could hear her voice in his mind. *Four horsemen shall come.* That was what she had told him. And the first would be called Death.

He made himself speak. "And what does this rider want?"

She was looking at him strangely, but she answered him quickly enough.

"He has not spoken nor moved since he arrived. Other messengers have come to the palace since the first. He waits, motionless on his horse, before the Arach Neben."

Gil sat there, his mind racing. What else had Carnhaina said? But Elrika interrupted his musings.

"You already know this, don't you?"

"No. Not really. Not at all," Gil said, still thinking of last night.

She gave him a long look from the other side of the table, but did not speak. Gil knew he had a friend here, but friends did not keep secrets. If he did not tell her what he knew, she would draw away from him, and suddenly that was the very last thing he wanted.

"Last night Brand took me to the Tower of Halathgar."

There was a reaction in the girl's eyes, and surprise was a part of it.

"The tower in the park? Isn't that where…" she trailed off.

"Yes. Whatever rumors you've heard are probably true, and far more besides."

He confided in her then. He was going to tell her just the basics, but instead he told her everything. He left nothing out, and she listened quietly. If she was surprised at Carnhaina's spirit appearing, as she must have been, she did not show it.

"Thank you for telling me that," she said when he was done. "It's a long story, and honestly, I'm not sure if I could have believed it except for the fact that the rider has come."

Gil knew what she meant. He was not sure that he would have believed it in her position at all.

Elrika took the last bite of her pastry and chewed it thoughtfully.

"So, what do you think the rider wants? Why does he just wait?"

Gil had not considered that, but instantly he knew.

"He's not going to try to come into the city. He's waiting for someone to go out to him. He's waiting for Brand."

Elrika looked at him. "I heard some soldiers talking. They said Brand was going to confront this thing, whatever it is. But I ignored them. I didn't think the regent would get involved personally. I thought he'd send someone."

Gil shook his head. "No. This whole thing reeks of sorcery, and Brand is the only one in the city who can deal with that."

They exchanged looks. They both wanted to go to the city wall and see the horseman, and they both wanted to see what Brand would do about it.

They did not even speak. It was in their eyes, and they stood and raced away out of the kitchen. Brand had probably already gone, so they would have to hurry to get to the city wall in time.

As they raced ahead Gil wondered about his bodyguards. In the confusion this morning he was unguarded, and that was unusual. He was not supposed to go out onto the streets without at least one Durlin, but it would take too long to find anybody now and get to the wall in time, even if they would take him there.

They raced out into the palace gardens and Elrika made for the streets.

"Wait!" he called. "It's too slow that way. We'll need a horse."

She stopped and looked back at him. "I don't know how to ride."

"Never mind," he said. "Follow me."

He led her to the stables and picked a quiet mare. Quickly he saddled her and got her ready, and then he helped Elrika up.

"She's quiet this one, but fast."

When Elrika was in the saddle he mounted and took the reins.

"Hold on tight!"

Her arms wrapped around him from behind and he nudged the horse forward into a trot. When they were out of the palace grounds and into the streets he kicked the horse into a much faster pace.

The streets were full of people. They always were, but riders were common and the city-folk kept a way clear on the side of the road. They did look though, for the mare rattled through at a fast pace and the clatter of her hooves over the cobbles was loud.

Gil felt a thrill run through him. He was free of the bodyguards, free of the palace and its constant undertone of politics. He was out in the city, a member of the population just like anybody else, and he had not felt that for a long time.

He knew that he led a privileged life. In many ways, he liked that. But it came with a burden of expectation. He would be king one day, and he did not really want to be. There was no freedom in that. It was a prison. He had learned as much from his grandfather, and it would shackle him to Cardoroth and his duty to rule the city and the realm. Such expectations left no room for what he really loved.

Even as he rode he felt the magic deep within him. It was always there, ready to stir at his will. He did not have much control of it yet, but that would come with practice and age. But in his case, as he grew older and took on more responsibilities, his opportunities to practice would lessen. What then of his dreams? To rule Cardoroth was something, but he could do more. If he mastered the magic, if he became a lòhren, he could be a force of good for the whole of Alithoras, not just one of its realms.

They raced through the streets and Gil was conscious of Elrika's arms wrapped tightly about him. She had not ridden a horse before, and she was scared. He could feel it in the way she gripped him. But at the same time he sensed that she was exhilarated too, and he was glad that he had confided in her.

They sped ahead. Tall buildings loomed over them. Dark alleys opened to either side, the sorts of places that were dangerous at night but were now filled with people and life. Above, red-tiled roofs glittered in the morning sun and high-arched windows flitted by. Gil did not hold back, desperate to get to the gate in time to see what would happen. He urged the mare forward, and she sprang ahead.

They saw the wall well before they came to it. It was the city's main protection. Throughout the history of Cardoroth no enemy had breached it, though, in the recent war, that had nearly happened. The people called it the Cardurleth.

Gil saw something ahead, and abruptly slowed the mare.

"What is it?" Elrika asked.

"Soldiers," Gil answered. "Lots of them."

He felt her lean sideways to look out past his body. "I see them. What are they doing?"

Gil was not sure. "They don't seem to be blocking the way. And many are mounted. I wonder…"

"What?"

Gil had gained a little more on them now. They only travelled at a trot.

"We're not too late," he said. "Brand rides at their head. I just caught a glimpse of him."

Gil deliberately stayed some distance behind. If he was seen now, he could be ordered back to the palace. Elrika did not say anything about his slowing down, and he guessed that she understood exactly what he was doing.

Nevertheless, they were nearly at the Cardurleth anyway, and within a few minutes Gil veered away down a side street. Then, he urged the mare forward again and they raced toward a spot he knew just a little away from the Arach Neben. It would take him far enough from the gate so that Brand would be unlikely to see him, and there was a wooden set of stairs leading up to the battlement where they would have a view of the encounter between Brand and the waiting horseman.

They came quickly to the wall. Once there they jumped down from the mare and Gil tied its reins to a hitching rail. Without hesitation after that, they raced up the stairs. The top of the battlement was filled with people, and Gil worried that he would not get a good view, but the two of them managed to press through until they came to a spot near the tower that protected the gate. There were some soldiers there who recognized him, and they made room so that he could see. Perhaps they would not have if they knew he was there without permission, but he was not going to tell them that.

They peered out over the battlement. The horseman was there, below them, motionless. They could not see much, and Gil was at first unsure why the people were calling this man a devil.

The horse he sat upon was black, but his robes were all of white. A white cowl covered his head, and he sat perfectly, even unnaturally, still. Then the black horse snorted, and Gil saw its nostrils flare. Inside, they were red raw, and a flicker of crimson flame curled within them. It was an eerie sight. But then he wondered if he had imagined it.

Even as the horse moved, the rider moved a little to keep his balance, and something stranger still occurred.

There were flies. A cloud of them rose, thickening the air, and then they landed upon the rider again and were still.

The rider stirred again, of his own accord this time. For a moment he looked around uncertainly, and then his gaze shifted to the Cardurleth, shifted straight to Gil, and fixed upon him.

Gil gazed back, enthralled. He could not understand it, but he sensed beyond any doubt that the rider knew exactly who he was.

And then, as if to confirm it, the rider lifted his arm and pointed right at him. A bent blade was in the figure's hand, sickle-shaped and wicked. The black metal of the strange weapon gleamed dully.

Gil felt a sudden stab of fear. It was overwhelming, but then the horse shifted its stance, the attention of the rider faltered, and Brand was there.

The regent came through the gate. His sword was sheathed at his side and in one hand he bore a white staff, the staff of a lòhren. He walked casually, seemingly unafraid, as though he strolled through the gardens surrounding the palace.

Gil felt movement beside him. Lornach was there. How the Durlin had found him, Gil did not know, but neither spoke. All that Lornach did was glance at him, and Gil felt suddenly embarrassed. He knew that he had done the wrong thing sneaking away from the palace, but there was no opportunity to say anything just now.

Below, a macabre scene unfolded that could not attract less than the full attention of every person who stood upon the battlement.

The rider urged his horse forward a few steps closer, approaching Brand and becoming more visible to those who watched. He came to a stop then, and pulled back his hood. The flies swarmed again, and a sudden stench filled the air.

Gil saw that the rider was no living man. Where a head should have been, there was a skull. Tufted hair sprouted from it. Skin clung to it in a few places and hung loose in others. Maggots fell from what had once been a face to ground. The eyes were writhing, bubbling pits of horror, and they fixed on Brand with unwavering hatred.

Some on the Cardurleth vomited. Many turned away. Gil closed his eyed and whispered, or perhaps merely thought to himself, he did not know, *Can Brand endure this?*

Lornach answered, or maybe guessed his thought. "Watch." His voice was hoarse, but there was a strange confidence in it.

Gil opened his eyes.

The rider was still again, but now he spoke. "I am Death," he said coldly, and his voice carried up to the battlement and beyond by some art of sorcery.

Brand gave a nonchalant shrug. "You certainly look dead enough."

There was silence for a moment, and then a grim laugh came in answer. It sounded like the rattle of bones rising from a deep pit.

"Death is where all living things go. Only I was there first. And I will be there last. And I will be there when no life is left at all, unchanged. Death is the only thing that survives death."

Brand straightened. "Well, you talk a lot – for a dead man. But let's get to the point, shall we? What is it that you want?"

The horseman smiled. His mount shifted its footing and neighed. Red fire flickered at its nostrils, curling up to lick at the air before its eyes. Gil was sure of it this time.

Brand remained relaxed and still, and Gil felt in awe of him. The presence of the rider was overwhelming even up on the battlement, yet Brand was right next to him and seemed unconcerned. What had that man endured in life to forge his will into a thing of such iron?

"I am Death," the rider responded slowly. "I want you. Many times have you cheated me, but you cannot cheat me forever. But this I will give you. It is a respite. If you take up the crown of Cardoroth, I will let you live … at least a little while longer."

A chill went through Gil. Carnhaina had also said that Brand would die unless he usurped the throne. What was going on here?

"I've been threatened before," Brand replied, and there was a new edge to his voice. "But my enemies are all dead."

The horseman laughed, and he seemed genuinely amused.

"Dead? Are they? *All* of them? I tell you this much, if no more. One at least lives."

"And who is that?" Brand asked.

"Ah! You will discover that. Eventually. But she knows you well. Yes, long has she studied *you*, and learned all your secrets."

"What does she want?"

"Revenge. And she shall have it."

Brand seemed puzzled, but his gaze did not leave his enemy.

"Revenge for what?"

The horse shook its head and pranced for a moment where it stood. The rider moved in the saddle to keep his balance and the flies swarmed and settled again.

"That is enough. I am done, for now at least. My message is delivered. Rule Cardoroth and live. Become king, and live. Anything else, and die."

Brand would have spoken more, but the rider and the horse both began to writhe. The stench that had come from them before increased. Maggots dropped to the earth like rain, and the bodies fell apart, seeping into the earth.

The rider was gone, but his words lingered, and doubt was in everyone's heart. What would Brand do?

The regent, for his part, studied the ground a moment as though in mild surprise and then casually turned and walked back through the Arach Neben. He disappeared from view.

Gil heard the crowd begin to whisper, and he felt eyes upon him. He was recognized by more than the soldiers now that people's attention was no longer focused below, and his name was on the lips of many. He felt suddenly very uncomfortable.

Lornach ushered him and Elrika away toward the back of the battlement.

"Time to return to the palace," the Durlindrath said.

Gil was worried. He exchanged a look with Elrika, and he saw fear in her eyes. It was not of the rider though, but rather of the words that had been uttered.

Without doubt, Gil trusted Brand. He trusted him with his life. The man was a legend. No one in the city could do what he just did, save perhaps Lornach or Taingern, the other Durlindrath. Yet still, between the words of Carnhaina and now this, Gil began to wonder. Brand would not be human if these warnings did not go to his heart. What man could ignore the same warning that came from friend and foe alike?

5. Other Servants than You

It was dark, and yet a glimmer of light came from the stone basin. The liquid within it moved, stirred to sluggish life by the images that played across its surface.

Ginsar watched. Her gaze was steady, but her pale hands trembled with excitement.

"It begins," she whispered.

Her acolytes, crowded behind her to try to see what she saw in the basin, did not answer. But their black-cloaked forms shuffled nervously.

Ginsar sensed their fear. She understood it, for the horseman that she saw in the basin, the horseman that confronted Brand, the horseman known as Death, had been one of their number. She had sacrificed him, and they had watched, and into the shell of his body she had summoned a force from without this world. And this she would do three more times.

The acolytes were right to be frightened. A smile played over her red lips, and she licked them in anticipation.

But her eyes never left the images she saw before her. She was drawn to Brand. Fascinated and repelled at the same time. Her hatred stirred, but she calmed herself and listened. By her arts she could do that, do what none of the acolytes could do, though they were sorcerers. And she liked what she heard.

Had she the power she would watch Brand all day, study his every move and word, and fuel her hatred of him. But she could not. She saw and heard only because her servant was there.

Somewhere in the dark of the chamber water dripped. It was always wet here. She hated it, but it was home. The cave had been home to her brother before, and to her master also. But they were gone…

Ginsar did not let her thoughts stray in that direction. She focused again on what was happening, and her heart leapt as she saw puzzlement on the regent's face. How she hated Brand! How she *loved* to hate him. It was exquisite to see him thus, pretending to be unafraid but all the while sensing that doom was catching up to him.

The horseman had delivered his message and seeped back into the earth. But he would come again, would rise for the confrontation that was inevitable. Inevitable as death itself.

The images ceased. The glow of light in the liquid faded away. It was still now, a dull red. And as the power was withdrawn from it, the blood in the basin began to congeal.

Light flared behind her, harsh and orange. One of the acolytes held a torch. With its flickering end he lit another set in the wall. On he would go, for many torches were needed to light this underground chamber. But her other servants gathered about her.

"It is done," she said. "The wheels are set in motion."

"Why not just kill them, man and boy both?" one of the acolytes asked.

Ginsar gazed at him and he shrank back. The acolyte beside the speaker looked at his brother. For a moment, a wicked smile played across his face, but then was suppressed. Oh, how she loved it. She could read their every thought, see their every strategy. They hated one

72

another, mistrusted one another and gloried in each other's errors. They vied for her attention, always seeking to be her favorite, and she loved that too.

Ginsar took a slow step forward. With her left hand she suddenly struck the acolyte who had spoken across the face.

The man reeled back, stunned by the raw force of the slap. He sagged to his knees and held his face in both hands, cowering.

With slow steps Ginsar approached. She stopped just before him, and drew herself up. There she towered above her servant, and he prostrated himself at her feet, whimpering.

Ginsar breathed in of the air, breathed in and trembled. How simple, how easy to snuff out this man's life. The temptation possessed her, made her heart flutter wildly. She lusted for it and her eyes blazed.

Slowly, she drew herself back. Not now. Not yet. His life meant nothing, but she would spend it wisely. A time would come later, would come for them all. They were only instruments to further her purpose, and when her purpose was achieved … she would celebrate.

She smiled. With a soft hand she reached down, caressed the man's cheek and drew him up to his feet.

When he stood, she lifted his chin and gazed into his eyes.

"Remember this. The power of life and death is mine. Brand and the boy will both die. But not just yet. First, they must suffer. They must suffer now, for after death they are beyond my reach."

The acolyte did not speak, but he trembled at the touch of her hand. She loved this power over him, over them all. They thought her mad, but they could not leave her. Thus they served, hating her and loving her by turns. Fawning for her favor, hating each other, desperate to learn from her store of secrets and power.

Ginsar let her hand drop from the man and turned away. She glanced at the basin. It was void of light now, a mass of thick blood, congealing. It would show her no more this day, but her plan was underway, and nothing could stop it.

Brand would die. He would pay for killing her brother. But that was not all. Her hatred for him was fierce. She would do anything to destroy him. She would destroy the world itself to get at him, but her hatred went deeper still.

She turned back to the acolytes and surveyed them. They were dark things, cloaked in black and filled with hatred like herself. They were sorcerers all, elùgroths, adepts of the dark powers that moved and substanced the world. But they had not her power, nor her knowledge, nor her foresight.

"Listen," she said to them. "I teach you the art that you desire to learn. I teach you elùgai. You know that in an age long since passed my own master was Shurilgar. From him I learned much, but the sight that I have, the foresight that blesses me, is my own. I was born with it, and I can see what was, and what is, and a measure what may yet be."

She paused to look at them, to gauge how much she should reveal.

"My sight stretches back to that age. My memory also, and I remember the founding of the kingdom men call Cardoroth. I remember it, and I remember also the rise of Carnhaina. It was she who taught my master defeat, and that was a bitter lesson to him, and to us who served him."

The elùgroths remained still, listening to her every word. The cavern was alight now with smoke-reeking torches, but the forms of the sorcerers remained shadows.

"That queen is long since dead, but her line endures. And while it lives, so too does our enemy. For though the queen is dead, yet still can she work through him to stymie my plans. I will not suffer that. I will not suffer her line to walk upon the earth. And I will not suffer Brand who killed my brother."

Her voice rose, and anger flashed in her eyes. "Think not that these things are unrelated. A battle is underway, the same battle that commenced a thousand years ago. Verily, Shurilgar was my master, and still is. We both serve the Dark, and Brand is of the Light. He is the key. Kill him, and the Light dies in Cardoroth. Kill him, and the death of the boy will follow. Kill him, and the long battle is at last won!"

There was silence when she finished speaking. The only sound was the constant drip of water. Into that quiet one of the acolytes, braver than the others, spoke.

"What now, Mistress?"

Ginsar smiled at him, rewarding his courage, showing him favor above the others.

"I have agents in the city," she said. Yet, seeing surprise on their faces, laughed. "I have other servants than you! But do not fret, my beloved. They are as nothing. They have no power, not of sorcery anyway. Yet still, they have uses."

She smiled again, to herself this time. She had set things in motion, perceived by the power of her second sight how they must proceed. It would not be long before revenge was hers, and the taste of that was sweet in her mouth. And when she closed her eyes, she pictured every detail.

"Now," she continued, "we must wait. Fate and human nature will unfold as they must."

She saw the puzzled looks on their faces, knew they did not understand. But they would.

As would Brand and the boy.

6. Dagger of the Duthenor

Gil was alone. After Lornach had seen him and Elrika back to the palace, they had all gone their separate ways. He was heading to his bedroom to study; a treatise on infantry tactics awaited him, and he treasured the feeling that walking the palace passages by himself and the prospect of several hours of uninterrupted study gave him.

Time alone was rare these days, and he enjoyed not having his every move watched by the Durlin who guarded him. It was true that they were subtle, that many of the city people and palace staff would not even have noticed how they trailed him, or spread out before him. But *he* did.

There had been much commotion after the horseman, and everyone's routines had been disrupted. There was sure to be a guard waiting outside his door when he got there, or one would arrive as soon as Lornach sent him. They were always outside his door, and he did not much like that either.

He walked through the empty passages, so different from how full of people they had been when news of the rider broke, and he heard a noise behind him. He turned and looked, but there was nothing there.

Moving on he came to a flight of stairs and ascended them. There was no further sound, but as he came into another passageway and strode down it, he heard a noise again.

Once more he turned, and this time he saw a man. Gil appraised him quickly, wondering who he was. He was not a soldier nor a palace servant. But he seemed nondescript and ordinary, so Gil gave a mental shrug and walked on. His room was close now.

It was a mistake, and he knew it instantly. No sooner had he turned to the front again than there was a flurry of movement from behind. The man had raced toward him.

Gil turned. He saw the flash of a blade, dull and frightful. He had no time to do anything except twist to the side. There was a thump, and the man seemed to bump into him. It was all too fast to be sure of anything.

Straightaway the man fled. Gil stood there in shock, unable to think clearly. Should he chase after his attacker, or call for help?

It was only when he felt the throbbing begin in his left shoulder that he realized he had been stabbed. He looked down and saw that blood stained his shirt and dripped to the floor. There, its blade glinting red, lay the dagger.

"Durlin!" he yelled, as he had been trained to do. His voice was loud, and there was a waver in it that scared him. "Durlin!" he called again, trying without success to keep his tone even.

He did not have to wait long. His room was only around the corner, and in a moment the bodyguard waiting there came rushing.

The man assessed the situation swiftly. His eyes were alert but calm, and Gil took reassurance from that. The Durlin took a cloth from one of his pockets and pressed it against the wound. Gil took hold of it and held it down himself.

"That way," he said, nodding with his head toward the stairs. "He went that way. Catch him!"

The Durlin looked at the stairs, and then back at him. "No," he said emphatically. "I'll not leave you unprotected."

Gil bit back his initial response. He had been unprotected just before. Then, as he thought about that, doubt washed over him in a wave.

Was it possible? Had it been arranged that no guards were present just so that an attempt could be made on his life? Was it possible that Brand could do such a thing?

Gil could not believe it. Yet here was the guard refusing to chase down the attacker. It was suspicious that the man would make no attempt to pursue an assassin, although it made sense that he did not want to leave him alone either. Gil calmed himself. He trusted the Durlin with his life, and Brand and Lornach and Taingern most of all. They would never betray him. None of them. Yet still, the doubt would not quite go away.

The Durlin lifted the cloth a little and studied the wound.

"You're lucky," he said. "Very lucky. It's only superficial."

The man studied the empty passage a moment, then pushed Gil's hand firmly against the cloth.

"Keep it pressed down hard," he instructed.

With a few quick strides he went to the stairs and yelled for help. It was not long before a palace servant came. They talked quickly, and Gil saw the eyes of the servant dart to him nervously several times as the Durlin gave him orders. Then the man was off, running down the stairs to get help.

The Durlin returned. He was cool, calm and professional as the guards always seemed to be. Brand chose his men wisely, and they were all loyal to him until

79

death. There seemed to be no emotion there, and Gil could sense nothing of what was going on in the man's head. That, and the Durlin's loyalty to Brand, did nothing to ease his doubts.

The man helped Gil to sit, and there they waited together. Gil tried to turn his mind to other thoughts. He would not think ill of Brand. The man was his hero.

He soon began to realize just how lucky he was. The attacker had been almost free to strike without fear of discovery or retaliation. Gil knew he had turned and disrupted the man, but his reaction had been too slow to offer any real resistance. Luck alone, it seemed, had directed the blade into his shoulder rather than his heart.

A moment later, Brand was racing up the stairs. How he had gotten there so quickly, Gil could not guess. It seemed impossible that the regent should arrive before other help. It seemed as though he had already been nearby for some reason … as though he had been expecting something to happen.

A chill ran through Gil, but as Brand approached and knelt down beside him, they looked into each other's eyes. All doubt left him then. There was concern there, and a depth of feeling beyond a regent for his charge. Brand's gaze was clear and steady, void of any deceit. Here was a man for whom his word was a bond. There was no betrayal in him, if Gil was any judge of character at all.

Yet a moment later surprise flashed over Brand's face. It was a look that Gil had rarely, if ever, seen before on the other's face.

He followed Brand's gaze and saw that it fell upon the bloody dagger on floor. Gil wondered why it should surprise him so, but before he could ask Brand had picked it up and slid it behind his belt.

"Why did you do that?" Gil asked. "Why did the dagger surprise you?"

Brand looked away and hesitated. Then he turned to Gil again.

"It's not an ordinary dagger. At least, not in this part of the world. I haven't seen its like in many years."

"I didn't see anything unusual about it," Gil said.

Brand looked quickly at the wound in Gil's shoulder. He had seen many such and knew, as did Gil, that even though it bled profusely it was not dangerous.

The Durlin kept the bandage pressed firmly against it, and Brand evidently decided that there was no reason not to talk while they waited for more help to arrive.

The regent withdrew the dagger from his belt. "See here," he said, tracing his fingers over the small pommel. This is shaped as a wolf's head. In Cardoroth, pommels are usually round. And look at this." He trailed his finger down the bone hilt. There were fine markings there, some sort of decoration or perhaps even writing. "This is scrimshaw. Many people carve in bone, but this pattern, this design … these markings are distinctive. It is a Duthenor dagger, somehow come from the far west, and I wonder how it got here for I'm the only one of my tribe to ever travel this far. At least, so I've always thought."

Brand looked away again, and Gil saw that the regent was puzzled. But the Durlin stirred uncomfortably. He must be thinking, just as Gil was himself, that he would have known if someone of his own race had entered the city. Surely, they would have contacted him, brought him news of his homeland, for it was well known in Cardoroth what his origins were.

Yet if there was no stranger in the city, no wandering Duthenor tribesman as Brand had one day been, then how

81

had the dagger come to be here? Unless it had been
Brand's ...

7. Worse than Death

Brand returned to the throne room after Gil's wound had been cleaned and dressed. The boy rested now in his room, but for himself, there would be no respite. Now was a time to think.

The throne room was quiet. But soon his advisors would come. Some were already there, those that he trusted most in all the world. They were few, but their opinions were vital. He was never afraid to act on his own, to do what was necessary, but likewise he was not scared to receive advice, to weight it up and judge it, to change his view or his course of action when a better way was shown.

He did not sit on the throne. Rather, he sat on a far less ornate chair beside it. The throne was for kings, and he was not a king.

Shorty was there, the man that most people knew better as Lornach. Taingern also. These were his oldest friends in Cardoroth, the men he had chosen to share the role of Durlindrath, his own previous title. But it was more than a title. It was an honor, a duty and a burden. It had broken men in the past. It had nearly broken him, but he had found a way through all difficulties to arrive at where he was today. And they were not there because they were his friends. They were there because they were great men, and he trusted them.

Arell arrived now, coming through the great doors of the throne room, as beautiful as always, her sharp eyes looking at him, reading his mood, discerning his thoughts as no other ever could. There was a trace of blood on her shirt, for she was the best healer in Cardoroth. The heir to the throne was not treated by just anyone.

A fourth person entered immediately after her. It was another woman. She was older than the rest, an old woman in fact. The others knew her, but not well.

The old king had told Brand that her name was Esanda. She preferred to be called Sandy though. Brand doubted anyone knew her true name, for secrecy was her stock in trade. She was the head of the king's secret intelligence service. Or, as the old king had told him once, the eyes and ears of the world. When she spoke, Brand listened. If he wanted to know something, she set her spies to find it out. He had come to rely on her, and he had also learned to trust her judgement. She knew better than anybody who was doing what, and why, and how best to influence them. And a king, or a regent, had need of such services.

They gathered before him. The Durlin at the door to the throne room knew no one else was coming, and closed it silently. They were alone, and Brand finally stirred.

He drew forth the dagger that had been used on Gil. It was clean now, the boy's blood removed, and Gil held it before him.

"You all know now that an attempt was made to assassinate the prince. This is the blade that was used. Look at it, and tell me what you see."

Their eyes fixed on it. The two men studied it professionally. They were warriors. Sandy looked, but gave no sign of what she thought. Arell gazed at it with distaste. She had seen the damage it had done, and remembered the many other wounds such weapons caused that she had healed, or tried to heal without success. Those men had died, and she thought of that now. He could sense her mood as well as she sensed his.

Shorty broke the silence, being direct as usual. "What of it? It's a dagger. That's all I see."

"Yes," Brand replied. "A dagger. Even an ordinary dagger, at least where it comes from."

Sandy sat back in her chair. "Well, it doesn't come from Cardoroth. You've just said as much yourself. But I don't think it comes from any other Camar city either. Not Camarelon or Esgallien or any of the others. So, where does that leave?"

Arell sat very still. She did not look at Brand when she spoke.

"I can guess," she said. "It's from the homeland of the Duthenor."

Brand knew that she did not want to say that. She understood well enough what it meant. She also knew that he would not have asked the question unless he wanted the information to surface.

"Exactly," he said. "It comes from the Duthenor. But I'm the only Duthenor tribesman in Cardoroth."

They all looked at him in silence. He saw trust in their eyes, and he knew that none of them thought he was responsible for what had happened.

He slid the blade of the dagger behind his belt. "So, what now?"

Sandy was the first to speak. "Likely enough, if there was another Duthenor tribesman in the city we would have heard of it by now. Nevertheless, I shall send word to all my … associates. If a tribesman has come into the city, I'll find out about it, eventually."

"It's a big city," Brand said. "Where would you even begin to look?"

"Well," she replied matter-of-factly, "the brothels are usually a good place to start. Foreigners always seem to end up there sooner or later. Usually sooner. Especially those who don't come from another city."

Brand smiled. "A good theory, but I didn't find my way to any such place when I first came here." He deliberately did not look at Arell.

"Maybe not, but as I recall you were pretty busy with other things at the time. Besides, you've never been an ordinary man."

"Nice of you to say so. Anyway, that'll take time. So, what do we do in the immediate future? Word of the dagger will get out. That, combined with what the rider at the gate said, will make people suspicious of me. There is a crime, and I have a motive."

Taingern scratched his chin. "The people may not be so quick to judge you as you think. They trust you, as do we all."

Brand thought about that. "Perhaps. Perhaps not."

"The aristocracy don't," Sandy said. "And they hate you to boot. They'll use this against you, try to destabilize your position. Indeed, for that matter, they must be the prime suspects in the whole business. How hard, after all, would it be to seek out such a dagger? A deliberate scheme to vilify you would hardly be beyond them."

Brand nodded. "That's true, but your ... associates keep a close eye on most of them. If they were planning some such thing, you would probably have heard a whisper of it by now."

Sandy gave him a guarded glance. "Maybe so. But there could be a conspiracy that I haven't yet discovered. I'll get my people to keep an even closer eye on things. Or a closer ear, anyway. It's marvelous the sorts of things a cleaning maid or stable hand can overhear, by accident."

Brand winked at her, but did not answer. Likely enough even his own servants were in her employ, one way or another. This was his way of letting her know that he knew.

He turned to Shorty and Taingern. "What of Gil? How will you ensure his safety? What happened today may well be tried again."

Taingern looked at Shorty, but it was the taller man who answered.

"We have no choice but to assume that another attempt on the prince's life will be made. We'll increase the guard on him."

"And," Shorty added, "we'll make sure that he's never left alone again. Ever."

Brand allowed himself a small smile. "Good luck with that. Gil is now of an age where he resents supervision, or guarding. He'll take it as a personal challenge to escape your watch."

Shorty shrugged. "I'll take it as a personal challenge to see that he's not successful."

There was not much more to say on the subject. Shorty and Taingern were the best at what they did. But Brand had one more thing to add.

"At the moment, you split the thirty Durlin between me and the prince. That must change. He's in the greatest danger at the moment, so all thirty Durlin will guard him."

"No!" Shorty said.

"Impossible!" Taingern added.

The taller man leaned forward in his chair. "You're the closest thing that Cardoroth has to a king. Should something happen to you, the realm would fall into turmoil. The aristocracy would be fighting in the streets to get one of their families on the throne, and our outside enemies could seize such an opportunity to strike. No, you must remain guarded."

Brand looked at them. He felt their loyalty as a palpable thing, and it moved him deeply. All the more because they had reason to doubt him just now, but did not do so. But though they were correct in what they said, there was a higher truth still.

"You're right," he said. "But you're wrong also. The boy needs you more than I do. I can defend myself, against blade or magic. Gil is still learning both."

The two Durlin began to argue, but Brand put an end to that straight away.

"I've made my decision, and it's final. The Durlin, all thirty of them, will guard Gil."

The two men looked less than happy, but they did not reply. Sandy, however, did.

"Don't be a fool," she said bluntly. "No one, no matter their skills, is immune to assassination. And it's possible that an attempt on the boy's life was made to provoke such a rash decision from you. You're predictable, at least in some ways, and a good assassin might have planned all this out."

Brand always admired that Sandy spoke her mind. She cared not a whit whether she spoke to kings, regents or peasants. She treated them all the same. Few could get away with such a thing, but she did.

"What you say is true, but I don't think you believe that's what's happening. Nor do I. I have a feeling that my greatest threat comes from the rider we saw at the gate. And the Durlin cannot protect me from that."

It was Arell who spoke next, and there was concern on her face no matter that she tried to hide it.

"The Durlin may or may not be able to protect you, but they should still know all there is to know. Tell them."

Brand hesitated, but he decided that she was right. So he quickly told them of his visit with the prince to the Tower of Halathgar and the warnings of the long-dead queen. When he was done, they looked at him in silence. There were few in Cardoroth who would believe such a tale, but those gathered here did. Shorty and Taingern because they had witnessed such things themselves, Arell and Sandy because they trusted. And because they had seen sorcery and lòhrengai in the not so long ago war that prepared them to accept the impossible as possible.

"Everything is vague," Sandy said into the ensuing silence. "Yet this much is clear. Cardoroth has enemies, and trouble gathers. It's said that the Forgotten Queen appears at times of great peril. She has given warning of these horsemen, and we have seen the first. An assassin stalks our city, and there is evil in the air. We know so little, but a battle of some sort is looming. We must prepare, and I sense that the assassin would be a good place to start. Learn his identity, and the rest will become clearer."

"That's true," Brand said softly.

Arell gazed at him, and there was sympathy in her eyes. "I know that you seldom speak of this, but it may help if everyone better understood why you left the Duthenor. Especially as it was a Duthenor dagger that struck Gil."

Brand shrugged. "You all know the story, at least in a general way. Most of you know that I have enemies in my homeland. But I have friends there too. In short, my father was chieftain of the tribe. When I was but a boy,

89

younger even than Gil, a usurper murdered my family. He would have murdered me too, but I escaped. He rules in my father's stead, supported by foreign warriors. Otherwise the Duthenor would have rejected him. I vowed that one day I would return and avenge my parents. The very fact that I still live must worry him. I'm the heir to my father's chieftainship, and if I ever returned I could fan the fires of rebellion."

Arell folded her hands in her lap. "That's reason enough that the Duthenor, or the one who now leads them, might seek to discredit Brand himself, or help others with that goal. Perhaps even try to kill him, if he could. But there's even stronger reason than that. Tell them, Brand."

Brand felt sadness well up in him. He remembered as though it were only yesterday the night his parents were killed. They were good people, deserving more from life than they had gotten. A deep longing to see them, to talk to them just once more, rose within him like a wave. He knew that Arell understood how he felt, and she was right to encourage him to speak of it.

"I was a fugitive," he said quietly, "but the people would have had me one day as their leader if they were given any choice. But neither I nor they had one. Having escaped the massacre, I was hidden by brave farmers as I grew, often moved from family to family and farm to farm because assassins sought me without stint.

"I realized as I matured that one day my luck would run out. One day, I would be found and killed, and those who sheltered me as well. Not yet full grown, but not a child anymore, I decided to leave the lands of the Duthenor to protect those who protected me. But I would not go without sending a message to the usurper.

"One night, I crept into the hall-yard that was my home in better days. Why would the guard dogs bark at someone who had played with them?

"I knew the ways of the old hall and picked a safe path among the sleeping men with slow steps until I came to the usurper's chamber.

"There, with great care and trembling hands, I opened an old chest and reclaimed the sword of my father, and his forefathers before him. With the ancient blade in my hands, I was tempted to kill the man who murdered my parents. But fear overcame me. I would not escape if I did that. Nor did I want to kill a sleeping man, even one such as he. Instead, I reached down and boldly slipped my father's ring, an heirloom of chieftainship, from his finger.

"But the usurper woke and gave a startled cry. Before it left his lips, I was already running. Men groped for their weapons all about. 'Awake! The hall is afire!' I cried, and in the confusion I somehow managed to slip away.

"The ruse did not last long, though. Soon I was pursued. On a ridge above the village, a sliver of the moon riding low in the midnight sky, I gave vent to my feelings. 'I am Brand! I will return one day, and death will come with me. I am the true chieftain, and when next I see the usurper my sword will slake its thirst for justice!'

"It was an empty threat, for I had no means to fulfil it, nor would I until I reached manhood, and not likely even then. I fled into the wilderness, but the story of my daring grew and spread among the people like a wildfire.

"Summer waned to autumn, and autumn turned to winter, and with my enemies ever pressing closer, I was forced to cross the frozen Careth Nien river. I nearly died then, several times.

"After that, I sought to lose my pursuers by traveling the many lonely miles toward Cardoroth. I thought that I had succeeded, but it may not have been so. Perhaps they followed me, made sure of my destination and returned to the usurper. But one such as he does not forget, nor less forgive, and I remember well the naked fear on his face when I fled the hall. No, one such as he does not forget. He hates me not just because of who I am, but also because of what I did."

Brand let out a long sigh and fell silent. They had all heard bits and pieces of this before, but not the whole thing. Only Arell had ever heard that.

No one spoke. They looked at him anew, reassessing him. He saw pity in some eyes, admiration in others.

Shorty eventually cleared his throat. "Perhaps it happened like that, your pursuers following you to Cardoroth. Or maybe not. Your fame has spread now, and stories of you must even have reached your homeland. That might explain why this usurper has only now taken action."

"Perhaps," Taingern said thoughtfully. "But the assassin went for the boy and not Brand. There's something more to this, something more complex than what I think this usurper would devise."

They all looked at him then. "The whole thing," Arell said, "is designed to make Brand look bad. Especially the words of the horseman."

Brand shrugged. "It could be. It's true that my Duthenor enemies would rather just kill me than anything else."

"Something else is going on, all right," Sandy said. "Perhaps someone is maneuvering to take the throne. If they kill the prince and discredit Brand at the same time, the way would be open."

"That could be," Brand said. "But I feel there is more to it than that. Much more. And none of these things explains the horseman. There was sorcery going on there, far darker and stronger than my enemies among the Duthenor or within Cardoroth possess."

"We'll never know," Shorty said. "Not unless we catch this assassin. First, we must better protect the boy. Then you, Brand."

Brand shook his head. "No Shorty. It's decided. The Durlin, every one of them, will guard Gil."

"You're too important," Shorty argued again. "If you die, the realm will fall into turmoil. The old king entrusted the regency to you for a reason. Cardoroth has many enemies. Only you can lead us."

"Well, that's not quite true. Gil is well liked by the people, and more importantly, by the army – at least the ordinary soldiers. Not only that, even though he's still young, he shows much promise. He has intellect and great courage. He also possesses magic. He'll make an extraordinary king, and his time is coming soon."

"All that is true," Shorty answered. "But as you just acknowledged, he shows *promise*. Promise is not enough. We need a leader, and we need one now. Cardoroth cannot afford to lose you."

"Enough," Brand said quietly. "I appreciate all that you say, but the Durlin will protect Gil. I'll look after myself."

Shorty sat back in his chair, and he said no more. He did not like it. None of them liked it, but that was the way it had to be.

Sandy looked at him, her expression inquisitive. "Just how good is the boy at magic?"

It was a simple question, but Brand liked it. He knew its purpose, and approved. Sandy, as ever, was thinking ahead. She wanted to know how effective Gil would prove as a king, for Cardoroth's enemies, when they attacked, employed not just armies but sorcery.

"As with all that Gil does, he learns swiftly. It doesn't matter if it's swordplay, or military strategy, or economic

93

theory. He grasps the concepts quickly. His skill with magic, with lòhrengai as it's properly known, is no different. He has great talent for it. In truth, he would be a lòhren if he was not born to rule Cardoroth."

Sandy considered that. "I've heard tell, that indeed, he would *prefer* to be a lòhren."

It was another good point, and Brand saw its purpose also. She continued to look to the future, weighing, evaluating, judging whether or not Gil would be a good king, whether or not he was best for the role.

"Gil makes little secret of that. He saw how kingship aged his grandfather and how responsibility weighed him down. He does not want the same thing to happen to him. He would prefer to use his talent with lòhrengai, to study it all his life and take it out into the world, to share his gift with Alithoras."

"And is that a quality to be sought in a king? A person who would rather be something else? I don't ask out of disrespect for the boy. I ask in the interests of Cardoroth."

Brand smiled. "That is the *best* sort of person to make king. The one who seeks such responsibility, who manipulates to achieve it, does not have the temperament to rule. Beware such a one as that."

The meeting ended soon after, and Brand was left alone in the throne room. He was alone often these days, and he thought much on the future of Cardoroth, and his own future, as he always did at those times. He had said that responsibility weighed people down. How true that was! Yet it had its benefits. You could not have the good without the bad.

His thoughts turned to Carnhaina. How well she would have understood all this. But the moment he thought of her he remembered her warning, or was it prophecy? Unless he took the throne, he would die. And the horseman had pronounced the same doom. One his friend and one his foe, but the warning from each just the same. It could not be ignored. It could not be acted upon.

Brand let out a long sigh and stood. There were no answers to be found, not today. But they were out there. And whatever they were, he knew that nothing was as it seemed. On that he would bet his life. But he had a feeling that his life was no longer his to bet. His destiny was become a pawn in a game that he did not understand.

He gritted his teeth and walked from the room. He would do what he must, and to *hell* with destiny.

8. Anything is Possible

Gil slept fitfully. His shoulder hurt, but the medicine that Arell had given him reduced that greatly. Far worse than the pain, though, was the dream.

It was not like before. Now, everything was vague. Yet he found himself in the forest again, and it was dark and gloomy. Shadows moved and shifted, and the black boughs of the trees swayed even though the air was still.

To the side was a lake. It was Lake Alithorin, though he had never seen it before. He turned his back to the water, and faced the forest. Things moved within it, dark things. They filled the woods, and they crept toward him.

Here and there he glimpsed a face, or the pale gleam of malevolent eyes. Now and then a twig broke, or dead leaves rustled beneath a furtive step.

Yet, this seeming army of enemies, though their ill will for him was palpable, waited. It was not long before Gil understood why.

Something bigger moved through the shadows. It made noise, not bothering to try to conceal its presence. Within a few moments the shape of the thing loomed. It was a horse. No, it was a horse and rider.

Gil took a step back. Death was come. The horseman paused, and the red nostrils of his mount glowed like living embers within the gloom. The rider slowly drew his sword, a bent blade, its wicked curve like a farmer's scythe.

The dark eyes of the rider fixed on him. They were hollow, hidden by shadow. They were pits of darkness, and yet still Gil sensed the movement of them. He knew there were no eyes there, but roiling maggots.

The rider grinned at him. Or maybe that was just the look of its skull-like face. And then Death charged. His mighty horse sprang forward, and the bent sword lifted high, high for a killing blow.

Gil had nowhere to go. He stood, still as a stone, bound by fear, or bound by the dream. The rider hurtled toward him.

Behind, Gil sensed the lake stir, and a light rose from it. Pale, silvery, mist-like. The rider faltered, and the nighttime sky shone brilliantly, suddenly awash with a countless multitude of stars. Halathgar twinkled brightest of them all.

Gil could not move. He sensed power behind him, and he felt that it was Carnhaina. Ahead, the horse reared and tore the air with its hooves. Grim and skeletal, Death sat astride his mount and his curved blade caught the light of the stars and turned it into wicked glimmerings.

For a moment, all was still. Then the forest, the rider and the silvery light all faded. Last to go was the mantle of the starlit sky, and then all was dark and Gil knew that he slept once more in his bed within the palace of Cardoroth. He stirred in his sleep, but did not waken.

The next morning, he trained with Brand. They could not spar because of Gil's injury, but he watched as Brand performed several routines, starting with warrior's exercises for the body that kept it supple, and finishing with a drill involving two knives.

Gil followed it all as best he could, studying and learning. At length, they sat upon a bench as the sun rose and talked about many things.

After a while, Gil turned the conversation to the horseman.

"How is it that you faced the rider so calmly? How do you prepare yourself for such a thing so that you don't become rooted to the spot with fear?"

The regent gave him an appraising look, his blue eyes gazing with sharp intelligence, and Gil wondered if there were any secrets this man could not discern just by looking. But whatever he had perceived of the reason behind the question, he said nothing and merely answered.

"This is how I approached it. I'll tell you all, because you may learn something valuable from it. Firstly, some advised me to ride out to meet him. The thinking was that no leader should talk to someone from a lower position. They did not think it seemly that a regent should stand to address a mounted messenger."

Brand gazed directly into his eyes. "I dismissed that. There's some logic to the sentiment, but it's more a matter of pride and show. Those things have no place in a potential fight. And that was what I was thinking of when I went through the gate on foot. If it came to a fight the horse would hinder my opponent, for such a conflict would not just be a physical battle but a contest of lòhrengai against elùgai. In that situation, I would be more agile on my feet than if I were mounted, nor would I need to worry about the safety of my horse, which would have no protection against such attacks."

That made sense to Gil. It was practical, free of self-importance. It was the outcome that counted, not the outward appearance.

"But how did you stay so relaxed?"

Brand smiled, if ever so slightly. "It was an act. Simple as that."

Gil was shocked, and the regent saw it. His smile widened.

"Of course it was an act. My guts were churning and my palms slick with sweat. How else could it be in such a situation?"

"But you looked so brave!"

98

"Brave? If there is no fear, then there is no bravery. Brave is doing something, doing something that you *fear*, not doing something when you know that you can succeed. Remember that."

"Then how did you manage to act like you weren't afraid?"

"Ah, that's a different thing altogether. Practice is the only answer to that. It wasn't the first time I've faced death or danger. My advice is not to seek it, *never* to seek it. But when it comes, look it square in the eye. A man makes many fears, draws them out of the very air and gives them form. But what will be, will be. You cannot worry about what *might* happen. That only gives your fears life. Instead, concentrate on the task at hand. Think of that only. Consequences will come after. That is their proper place. If you think of both the task at hand as well as the future, well, then you're fighting two battles instead of one. And likely enough you'll win neither."

Gil knew there was more to that advice than he understood. But, as Brand always asked, he'd remember those words. As time went by he would understand them better.

"What else did you do?"

Brand shrugged. "Not much else, really. Mentally, it was just a matter of not showing surprise, no matter what was said. Never let an opponent surprise you, or at least never give him confidence by letting him see that he has done so."

Gil asked the obvious question. "And what about physically? You've mentioned why you went out on foot, but what else did you do?"

"Only the basics really. Most of this you know already. Firstly, I ensured that my right hand was free. So, when I

99

crossed my arms to make it appear that I was unconcerned, my right hand rested on the outside of my left arm, rather than trapped *beneath* it. It's only a slight difference, but it allows for swifter movement, no matter how slight."

"Did you use the sun?"

"Not really. By necessity, I came through the gate and it faces west. The sun would have been in the rider's eyes, but it was morning and the tall wall of the city put us both in shadow from the rising sun."

"What about the terrain? Could you positon yourself on higher ground and the rider on lower?"

"That, I tried. But the road there is flat. There was a pothole, but the horse stepped aside from it."

Gil could think of nothing else to ask, but he knew there would be more.

"What else did you do?"

"I observed if the rider was right or left-handed. And I think he was right-handed – at least the positioning of his scabbard on the left hip indicated that, along with the fact that he held the sword in his right. The latter doesn't mean much though. A trickster might attempt to deceive you that way and swap the weapon to his other hand during a fight. But he's much less likely to alter the position of his scabbard to reinforce that trick. So, I stood ready to move to the left of the horse where the rider would have less mobility and power in his strikes."

Brand paused, considering his actions and evaluating them.

"Probably the most important thing in such a situation is this. Don't let your opponent see doubt. You must be confident, supremely confident. It's not a matter of bragging, or a case of *false* confidence though. Those things are useless. It's a matter of trusting in yourself, of believing in yourself. And that only comes through training and practice. You have to do the hard work first. You must sheath your mind with an iron-like determination. Decide what you need to know in your life, and then acquire those skills. It's as easy, and as hard, as that. When you've done so, then anything is possible."

Gil had much to ponder. Soon, though, their training session ended. He went then to the kitchens in search of breakfast. No sooner had he sat down than Elrika approached, and he pulled out a chair for her. Suddenly, he wanted the company of someone his own age. Talking to Brand was great, but sometimes it made him feel a hundred years old. And even if he ever did live to be that age, he wondered if he would understand all that the regent told him.

Between helpings of buttered bread, ham and well-aged cheese, they spoke.

"Were you scared of the rider?" Elrika asked.

Gil thought about that. He had been, especially when the horseman looked straight at him.

"A little," he said. "But I knew Brand was his match. There wasn't even a fight. I think the rider was scared of *him*."

Elrika seemed to consider that. "Maybe," she said. "Or maybe their time to fight hasn't come yet. I get the feeling that it will, though."

Gil ate more bread. He had also had that feeling, and it worried him for some reason.

"How's your shoulder?" Elrika asked.

Gil knew that the bandages were visible above his collar, but he wondered how she had so readily known that he was wounded.

"There are no secrets in the palace," she said. "I heard last night that you had been attacked. Do they know who it was yet?"

"No. Not yet." He said nothing about the Duthenor dagger, but he did not doubt that rumor of it had also spread.

"It may have been the aristocracy," she ventured.

Gil finished eating and leaned back in his chair. "It could be. They hate me enough. And I hate them, for the most part."

"Really? Why's that?"

He thought about the reasons he had, and he wondered if he should tell her. But it felt good to confide in someone.

"Mostly," he said, "because they call me elùgrune. Or nightborn."

"Does it really worry you that much?"

He wanted to say no, but did not. Instead, he looked at the marks on his hands.

"In truth, it does. I *hate* it."

Elrika seemed to consider that. "I can see why, but if it weren't that, then it'd be something else. They try to intimidate you because of *who* you are. Not *what* you are. But anyway, you should know that not everybody thinks the marks on your palms are evil. Without Carnhaina, we would long ago have been destroyed. My dad says the same sign is in many places in the city. He saw it once in the palace itself, in an old store room. It had been closed for many years but opened one time when an excess of grain had to be stored. He said it was a strange room, but the mark of the Forgotten Queen was everywhere inside it."

Gil thought that he knew every room in the palace, but he had never seen that one. He wondered how that was possible.

"Will you show me where it is? I'd love to see it."

The girl looked at him seriously for a moment. "Of course," she agreed. "But it'll have to be later. My father has chores for me to do now."

He smiled at her. "I know the feeling. The chores never seem to end."

She left soon after that, and Gil filled in time wandering about the palace in search of his attacker. He found nobody who looked like him, and grew tired of the attempt. Almost, he felt sorry for the Durlin who trailed him wherever he went, closer today than they had ever been before. He did not like it, even though he understood it.

In the afternoon, he made his way to the training yard where Shorty had taken the place of the Swordmaster. He would not be able to join in, but he could still watch and learn.

He noticed that some of the usual boys were not there, but most were. Unfortunately, Turlak, the older boy who had recently caused him so many problems was one of the ones who had returned. Gil wondered why. He had been the old Swordmaster's favorite, and surely must now hate Shorty.

Shorty himself showed up moments later. He demonstrated a sword form that none of the other boys had ever seen before, and then he led them through it step by step.

The form was swift, unbelievably so when Shorty demonstrated it, and it seemed designed to teach the type of footwork that enabled fast and powerful strikes. There were leaps, squats and pivots, and Shorty explained as he took them through it that it was all about learning to use the body first and that a sword was only an extension of it.

"You'll learn the form," he told them, "and then break it down technique by technique. After that, you'll put the moves into practice on each other with the wooden swords. Finally, you'll introduce the techniques into your sparring sessions."

Gil listened carefully and watched Shorty very closely. There were many techniques here that he had not seen before, but he recognized some that Brand taught, even if there were slight differences. This perplexed him, but after a while he realized that the differences were only to be expected. Brand was tall and Shorty was short. *Make every technique your own*, Brand had often told him. Now he understood that advice better. Every individual was different, and no matter how sound a technique was in itself it must be adapted to suit differences in height, strength, speed, temperament and the like.

Gil was pondering this when he saw a finely dressed man approach. He knew him for the father of one of the boys in the class, and also as an earl.

The man beckoned his son over and then called out to Shorty.

"A word with you."

Shorty strolled over. There was that look to him that he always bore, relaxed and yet somehow ready for anything. Gil had seen it many times, and he also noticed the ever-so-slightly narrowed gaze that signaled intense concentration.

The earl pointed at his son, and light glinted off several diamond rings.

104

"I have come to withdraw my boy from this school."

Shorty looked at the man steadily. "As you wish."

The earl seemed slightly taken aback by Shorty's acceptance of the situation, but he continued in his smooth voice.

"I will do you, sir, the courtesy of telling you why."

"Somehow, I rather thought you would," Shorty answered.

The earl frowned at him, but Shorty had not really said anything offensive, though the tone of his words made it clear that he was not concerned with anything the earl had to say.

The boy's father crossed his arms, and the diamonds flashed again against his black silk shirt.

"You do not seem, sir, very interested in learning why."

Shorty gave a slight shrug. "I already know why."

The man seemed less and less certain of himself, but he drew himself up and continued.

"I do not believe so. This is what I would have you understand. The regent, though perhaps I should say *King* Brand, has promoted many uncouths such as you. But know this!" Here, his annoyance at Shorty began to show. "Brand will not endure. One day we will be free of foreign rule, nor do we accept that the whelp of a previous king, marked by the stain of an ancient ancestor's dabbling in the dark arts, and to whom Brand teaches his foreign ways, will rule Cardoroth either. Other families of ancient and noble lineage will one day see their time under the sun…"

The man stuttered to a stop. Shorty had changed while he spoke. No longer did he seem carefree. Now, there was a look of cold death in his eyes.

"Insult me if you like," Shorty said. "I've heard the same words from many mouths before this. Insult Brand, if you will … he cares less about what you think than I do. Your opinion is as nothing to him, for though you walk on two legs you're not a man. While Brand and I risked our lives in the last war to save this city, you drank fine wine and buried your wealth in hidden vaults beneath your mansion. Don't deny it! Brand knows exactly who you are, and many things about you that you would prefer to keep secret. But if you insult the heir to the throne, infer that you conspire with others to supplant him … then that is treason."

Shorty, slowly and deliberately, placed a hand on the hilt of his sword. A hush settled over the practice yard, and no one even seemed to breathe.

"So, was that treason my Lord, or did I mishear you? Speak swiftly! Or, in case you've forgotten, I'm not just Durlindrath but also the old king's champion. As such, I may just now deliver the king's justice. And that will be a duel that ends with my sword in your guts."

If it were possible, the silence deepened. The earl blanched. Though he wore a sword, he, along with everybody else, knew that he was no match for the Durlindrath.

With great care the earl clasped his hands together behind his back. He wanted to ensure there was no mistake. He had no intention of fighting. Then he smiled slyly.

"It is not treason to repeat hearsay rumored on the streets of the city. Good day to you, sir."

With a dismissive nod he turned his back on Shorty, drew his son around with him and began to walk away.

"Coward," Shorty said. His voice was quiet but clear.

The earl paused in mid stride, and then pretended not to hear the deadly insult. He walked away.

The class continued after that, but it was subdued. Gil could not help but wonder if what the earl had hinted at was true. Did the aristocracy really believe that Brand would usurp the throne? And for their part, were they really trying to maneuver so that one of their own would start a new line of kings? If either of these things happened, what of him? A prince, not yet come to manhood, had no place in either situation.

9. A Door to the Past

That night, Gil slept. And for the first time in a long while his dreams were not troubled. He woke early, and unusually hungry. Even though it was one of his days off, and he had no training with Brand, nor chores nor any study to do, he got out of bed while it was still half-dark and headed to the kitchens.

Of course, there were two Durlin at his door when he opened it. They had been there all night, and he felt sorry for them. Guarding a room was a boring duty. But they seemed resigned to it, and after a perfunctory greeting they followed, quietly, but very closely.

He went to the bakery area, and sure enough Elrika was there as he hoped. She spotted him and smiled, knowing straight away what was on his mind.

She brought him over a meat pie and a pastry, and they sat together and talked while he ate. She would have noticed the two Durlin, but she said nothing about them.

"So," she said in a whisper when he was finished with breakfast. "Is today the day?"

She had made no comment about the Durlin, but obviously she did not want them to hear what was being discussed, and Gil was grateful. What they were about to do, the room she would lead him to with the mark of Halathgar, was somehow intensely personal. He respected the Durlin, all of them, but this was for him alone, and for his friend.

"Are you free today?"

She smiled. "I am, until lunch at any rate. Let's go before my dad sees me and decides I'm being too idle."

Gil had not been sure if she would be available, and suddenly things were happening very quickly. A sense of anticipation rose within him, and with it came some nerves. This would be something new, perhaps even something that Brand did not know about. Although lately he had begun to wonder if Brand was not somehow aware of every single thing that happened in Cardoroth.

They left the kitchens, the silent Durlin close behind them. Down they went, working their way through corridors and descending flights of stairs.

Elrika leaned in close and whispered to him. "Do you want to leave your guards behind?"

Gil enjoyed the feel of her so close to him, but it made him nervous too.

"Yes, but I don't see how. We can't just try to run away from them."

She flashed him a smile. "Just be ready, and follow me when the time comes."

Her quick words only made him more uneasy, but he dared not ask any questions. The Durlin were only a dozen or so paces behind them. Not so close as to get in his way, but close enough to reach him within a few heartbeats if he needed help. And when other people were around, they drew closer.

They descended another set of stairs, and then entered a long corridor. Gil could sense Elrika suppressing excitement beside him. She seemed to be nearly jumping out of her skin, and he knew that whatever she had in mind was going to happen soon. Nevertheless, she did not quicken her pace, and continued to walk with the same measured stride that she had used since they began.

109

They turned left at a bend in the corridor, and there before them was a landing and several stairways rising and falling from it. This was a juncture point that Gil knew, a place where servants came to have quick access to most parts of the palace. He had been here before quite a few times, so what Elrika did next surprised him.

Suddenly, she was all motion. With swift hands she reached out and opened a panel in the wooden wall that Gil had never even seen before. It was small, but she jumped though it and pulled him in after. Quickly she closed it, and there was a faint click and then silence. In the dim light he saw her put her fingers to her lips.

It was only a moment before the Durlin came around the corner and reached the same spot. Gil could sense their astonishment even though he could not see them, and then there was the sound of running feet and yells.

The Durlin raced to the stairs, checking them for any sign of their charge, but Elrika took his hand and led him carefully to the left. Immediately, they were on a new flight of stairs, their own pathway to freedom that was hidden from the outside world. In moments, the clamor of shouting receded, and soon after their eyes adjusted to the dimness.

"Where are we?" he asked.

Elrika shrugged. "Sometimes servants don't want to be seen. There are several staircases like this throughout the palace. They offer an occasional escape from the condescending gazes of the aristocracy when we just want to go about our business. And sometimes it provides a means of communication between two parties who would prefer – who would like to keep their visits to one another's rooms … that is, people who really just don't want anybody to see them, er, communicating."

Elrika's quiet voice trailed off and Gil blushed. He was glad of the dark, and neither of them spoke for a while as she led him downward.

His thoughts wandered back to the two Durlin. He would apologize to them later, and he would explain to Shorty and Taingern that it was not the fault of the guards. He did not want to see them get in trouble.

There seemed to be more light now, or perhaps their eyes continued to adjust. At any rate, he glanced over at Elrika. He found that she was looking at him. There was a curious expression on her face. It was almost like she knew what he was thinking, because her expression seemed to indicate that she understood well enough why the Durlin had been following, and she knew also why he wanted to be free of them. She *understood*, and that somehow strengthened the bond between them.

Down they went to the very bottom of the palace. There were no doors, no corridors, no mothing. There were only the stairs. They were narrower than the usual stairs in the palace, and in need of repair in several places, but still safe enough.

After a while, it grew darker again. There was very little noise, and Gil began to have a sense of how a place such as this was a refuge for the servants. They should not need one, but they did. Once again Gil appreciated Brand's foresight. His training, his exposure to the aristocracy and to commoners alike, was opening his eyes to things that he would not otherwise have seen.

It grew darker still, and he began to have misgivings. What if he ran into the assassin again in a place like this? Should he really have left the guards behind? There was no help for him down here if something happened.

111

Elrika reached out and took his hand. "Nearly there," she said, once again seeming to sense his feelings.

They shuffled along a little while longer through the dark, and then it began to lighten once more. Soon they came to a recess. The stairs ended, and a blank wall began. But Gil was not surprised this time when Elrika reached up and placed her hand on the timber. There would be another hidden panel there, but she did not open it straight away. Instead, she placed her face against it for several long moments and listened.

"I can't hear anybody outside," she said.

Slowly, she tripped the mechanism that held it in place. There was a click, and she peered carefully through the slit in the wall that had appeared before opening it up all the way.

They stepped through into a normal palace corridor, and Elrika closed the panel behind them.

Gil knew where they were. He had been here too. He had thought he had been everywhere in the palace, though that belief was now shattered. Still, he remembered this corridor well.

"The wine cellars are beyond," he said.

Elrika nodded, and then leaned in close to speak softly.

"They are, but there's usually a caretaker down here. We'll want to avoid him. Otherwise he'll want to know what we're doing and where we're going."

She led him forward, her shoes soft and soundless on the floor, and he followed like her shadow.

To each side there were doorways. Elrika carefully scrutinized each entry before passing the openings. Brand saw rooms filled with cheeses, and others with hams that hung from the ceiling. Yet others were filled with cured sausages, hanging and drying in the cool air. There was a

112

strong scent of smoke, one of Gil's favorite smells, and he was suddenly hungry again. But Elrika led him on.

They came now to the wine cellars, and these branched off down several narrow tunnels. There were racks against the wall and endless bottles and flagons. Gil was not even sure if they were man-made corridors or just caves beneath the palace. Either way, it was growing dark again, but they both paused in mid stride as a shadow moved at the far end of one of those long wine tunnels. There was a shuffling sound too, and then a husky voice coughed.

"The caretaker," Elrika breathed into Gil's ear.

They dropped slowly into a half crouch and moved carefully past the opening. There was another cough and a few muttered words as the caretaker spoke to himself.

They had not been seen, and they moved quickly and quietly ahead. They came swiftly to the end of the corridor. There, an ancient door barred their way. It was, perhaps, of oak, but it was an aged thing now, still solid no doubt, but covered by mold and stains.

Elrika glance behind her once, and then took hold of the ancient brass door handle. It was dull and dirty. Slowly she turned it, and then pulled the door open. The hinges creaked in protest, but not loudly.

They slipped through and Elrika closed it behind them. Then they waited a moment in the dark, listening. The caretaker may have called out, having heard some noise. Or maybe he just spoke to himself. Whatever the reason, they heard his voice briefly and then it grew deadly silent. Gil could hear nothing after that, nor could he see much.

Elrika moved in the dark beside him. There were several scratching sounds, and suddenly there was a flash of light. She had lit the wick of a candle, and she held it up before her face.

Gil smiled at her. She had been prepared for this, but a moment later he looked around, keen to see the nature of the room she had led him into.

Shadows danced and slithered. The air was heavy with the smell of ancient smoke and dust. Wooden crates, perhaps centuries old, slowly fell apart in the endless dark and there was a sense of antiquity. No matter how much the city had changed above, this place had not altered in many, many years, nor ever would. No one came here, and if they did so once in every few decades, they left again, happy to leave it just as it was.

The two of them moved forward through the wreckage of dilapidated crates and the rotting remains of hessian bags. No doubt these were the remnants of some grain sacks from the time that Elrika had spoken of. There was nothing in them now but dust and old shadows.

They came to the middle of the room and Elrika held the candle above her head. Eerily, the ceiling sprang into view. Cobwebs hung from it. Plaster and paint cracked and shriveled over it. But there, in the very center, a brilliant blue constellation glittered. Halathgar. The Seal of Carnhaina. If time had touched the rest of the room, it had left that paint alone. Like eyes, the twin stars stared down from above, and Gil had the unnerving feeling that they watched him.

Elrika shivered beside him, and he reached out to hold her hand. The one that lifted high the candle trembled, and Halathgar twinkled in the shivering light.

Now, Gil looked about him, drinking in the room, breathing in its age and the dust and the cobwebs as forgotten as the years that passed by in endless succession of dark days and darker nights. Now, he saw more images.

The queen was there, Carnhaina herself. There was no mistaking her, nor the spear in her hand, even if the ages had chipped and peeled away at the paint. There were other images as well, of things that Gil did not recognize, or so damaged by time that they could no longer be made out with certainty. And bright Halathgar was there in several more places, though smaller and less impressive than the representation on the ceiling.

A good while they spent there, just observing these signs from a past age, awed by them and their antiquity. They did not speak, but often their eyes met and Gil saw as much wonder in Elrika's as no doubt was in his. This was something special. No matter that it had been locked away and forgotten by most in Cardoroth. Maybe even many in the city would not care. But Gil did. This was something that connected him to his great ancestor. Here, no doubt, she must have stood herself in a time that was long ago. And the artist who had made these images had also once been alive. He had crafted her semblance, but to do so with the accuracy that he had he must have seen her and heard her speak. He had conversed with her. Time had buried that event in a mass of years, but the evidence of the moment still endured.

Gil exchanged another glance with Elrika. They had explored it all, had peered at every image. They knew they would come back another time, but the outside world pressed. The Durlin would be looking for him, and it was time to go and to face the consequences of his disappearance.

He took a final look at the room, but something tugged, ever so faintly, at his senses. He was puzzled, for he had never felt such a thing before. Elrika raised an eyebrow at him, sensing his hesitation and that something was happening, but did not voice a question.

Gil calmed himself. He breathed slow and deep as Brand had taught him. He allowed his mind to open, to expand, to become one with his surroundings. And the tugging sensation increased. More, he knew its source.

He glanced at the far wall of the chamber. It was covered in dust and grime and the disintegrating threads of an ancient spider web. There was an image on it of Halathgar, worn and faded. He had looked at it several times so far, but now he knew that it was the thing that triggered his instincts. There was something else about it too that was unusual: even though it was a constellation, it was placed on a wall. All the others were on the ceiling, which seemed a more natural location for them.

He went over a for a closer inspection, and Elrika came with him.

"What is it?" she asked finally.

Gil shook his head. He did not know. "Something…" he said absently.

The image was chest high. He reached out with his right hand and brushed away the spider web and some of the dust. He felt a tingling in his palm.

He paused a moment. An idea occurred to him, and he wondered if it was a wild and stray thought born of imagination, or if his instincts were seeping through to his conscious mind. He decided to put it to the test.

Slowly, hesitantly, he brought up his left hand and pressed it against the second star. Instantly, he felt a thrill of power in both palms. There was lòhrengai in this wall, ancient and slumbering, but brought now to wakefulness.

Stone ground against stone, a rumble as though the earth itself moved in its sleep. A crack appeared, straight and vertical. It was not natural, but made by the art of man. And then the wall moved.

Gil flinched and withdrew his hands. The wall split in two, sliding to the left and the right, leaving a doorway. Dust puffed out of the two corners of the room where sections of wall slid a foot or so into some hidden recess.

It was dark as night beyond the door. Silently, Elrika held up the candle. By its light they saw a narrow tunnel, and beyond was a set of wooden stairs. They seemed ancient, and Gil wondered how long since anyone had seen them or trod the path they made.

"They're no servant's stairs," Elrika said softly. "Where do they go?"

Gil straightened. His apology to the Durlin would have to wait.

"Let's find out." He looked at her, and she gazed back at him. He saw fear there, but also a curiosity as great as his own.

10. Hail, Master!

The elùgroths gathered around her as moths drawn to a flame. Ginsar reveled in their adoration. It pleased her as much as their fear. And, right at this moment, she sensed both swirl in the dark air with a force that intoxicated her.

She, the greatest among them – she, sole disciple left living of the great Shurilgar, was about to perform a summoning that defied the laws of the earth. Well might lesser creatures tremble as they milled about her, for tonight was a night like no other. It would be like no night they had ever seen.

The elùgroths fell back as they reached the shores of the lake. They knew this was where the summoning would happen. They stood silent, their bickering, their petty rivalries and their intricate schemes forgotten; at least for the moment.

She stepped forward a few paces by herself. It was the dark hour before the beginning of dawn. The night was dying, but the sun had not yet birthed the slow graying of the sky. It was that moment when the world stood poised in transition, when there were worlds within worlds and the power that governed all things ebbed. Dark was the pine forest behind her, its shadows stalked by death, by the hunted and by their hunters. Ahead, the water of the lake was impossibly still. A silvery light was on it, gleaming and glistening like dew laid down by the moon. But there was no moon.

Ginsar studied the water. It was beautiful, or so she had been told. To her, beauty was power and obedience. Nevertheless, whatever the lake was now, it was about to change.

She straightened and stood to her full height. As she did so, those behind her cringed. They were scared, and well might they be. But she paid them no heed. Out, out her mind spread, out over the water. She plumbed its depths, became one with it, flowed with its currents and felt everything between the muddy bottom that cupped it to the mirror-like surface that topped it.

Beneath the dark fringe of the forest four riders appeared. She did not see them, but rather sensed their presence. She had brought them into existence and knew at all times where they were and what they were about. They were hers to command, and yet they made her uneasy.

She turned her mind to the deed at hand. Her mouth moved, and in a whisper that slowly grew she chanted. Her words filled the air, and then gained substance and descended into the water. Words and power were one, power and words melding until her thoughts came to life.

Fire spurted beneath the water. There were no limits to her strength, and she felt the intoxication of her magic as a wine that coursed through her blood. It was joy and bliss and it gave life and purpose to her being. It would do anything for her, and she anything for it. It was alive.

Once again, she felt a stirring of unease and suppressed it. At her thought the fire turned scarlet and then green and then blue. She shifted between them in a frenetic rush, playing with her power, toying with the forces that moved and substanced the world. She reveled in it, and yet knew at the same time that there were those who would say that such an uncontrolled use of the power reflected an uncontrolled mind, a mind that was insane, a mind where the power controlled her and not her it.

She made the fire shiver with a thought and laughed. Fools! All of them were fools. I am sane and the rest of the world is wrong!

Her hands grew rigid and her fingers stabbed down. Fire plunged into the depths of the lake, down to the muddy bottom and the solid earth beneath. Nothing happened. The world became suddenly still. Then a great chill descended. The stars glittered above and frost glistened on the long needles of the pine trees.

Suddenly, the water of the lake seethed. It hissed and boiled and thrashed, growing angry. The water tossed and turned like a man gripped by a terrible nightmare. It writhed with forces seeking escape, forces that she had called into being. The water became fire, turning and shifting to her every thought.

A noise began. It was not the splash of water nor the cackle of fire. It was a desperate wailing. And there were words within it, angry words, swearing and curses. There was pleading and threats and screams and promises of dark deeds.

Then the faces appeared. The fiery water showed them all. Staring faces. Cruel faces. Kind and goodly faces. There were people and monsters and things born of other worlds. They tried to rise up into the air and escape the lake, but the water churned and pulled them down just as easily as it brought them up from the netherworlds that were their origin.

Ginsar laughed. Her fingers stabbed again and then clawed at the air. A swirling vortex formed far out in the lake. From this a figure rose, tall and splendid, robed in fiery water and crowned with white froth.

The sorcerers behind Ginsar fell to the ground. Power throbbed in the air, and the figure, mantled in awe and dread majesty, drew a shuddering breath and lifted high its arms. Then it bent, and lowering a hand into the churning water upon which it stood, drew up a lesser figure to stand in its shadow.

Together, the two figures glided over the water and came toward the shore, shadowy robes billowing in otherworldly air.

Ginsar let out a breath between clenched teeth, and it turned to a white plume in the frigid air. The summoning was complete. As the dead who were called forth approached, the white sand at the margin of lake and land turned red as though wetted by the blood of all who had ever died.

She shuddered and dropped to her knees. "Hail!" she cried in a trembling voice. "Hail, master and beloved!"

Away in the forest nothing moved. But the trunks of some of the trees, gripped by frost and frozen, burst with deafening cracks.

11. The Voice of the Past

Gil and Elrika followed the stairs. They led back up into the palace, but where they would finish was a mystery beyond guessing.

The timber was rickety, and dust covered everything in deep layers that had laid undisturbed for years beyond count. Gil doubted anybody had been this way in centuries. The dust seemed thick enough for that, but there was no way to tell for sure.

The stairs were narrow, and they were hemmed in by high balustrades of carved hardwood. The two of them walked together, forced close by the railings. Gil did not mind.

Elrika ran her hand over a balustrade. The dust peeled away revealing timber that was deep red with a fine grain.

"So much dust," she said, "but once this was an expensive staircase. It might be narrow, but the timber is far better than what was used in the servant's stairwells. And the craftsmanship is better too. All of this means something, you know."

"What do you think?" Gil asked.

She shot him a look. "You know what it means."

It was true. They had gained entry by lòhrengai, and not just lòhrengai but by the Seal of Carnhaina. This was a passage designed for the great queen, and possibly it was a secret. No, he decided. It *was* a secret, even in her time, and the secret had died with her, else the stairwell would have been in everyday use.

The walls around them turned from wood to stone. It seemed to Gil that although the stairs remained the same the passage that they took had been built at different times. That was possible, of course. Carnhaina had not founded the city. Her father had done that, and it may be that she had furthered the construction of some secret tunnel. None of that, though, explained its origin in the first place. What need had there been for a secret tunnel at all, whenever it was built?

Whatever the case, the fact that the walls were of stone gave Gil the idea that they were now somewhere in the actual outer wall of the palace. That made some sense, because it would be easier to keep the construction secret that way. On the other hand, it limited the number of places that the stairwell could lead.

Yet, evidently, it did lead to other places. From time to time they came to doorways. These, they did not open. At least if they kept to the main stairwell they could not get lost. Moreover, they both had a feeling that the stairs led somewhere important. They would keep on following them up and to whatever place that was.

They went ahead. The stairs grew slightly wider now, and were in better repair. The dust, however, remained just as thick.

"We must be high in the palace," Gil ventured.

"At the very top, I think," Elrika answered. "The stairs cannot go on much longer."

She was correct. Very soon after they came to a chamber. It was, at least it had been, well decorated. Old hangings rotted away on the walls. Gil's eyes were drawn to marks on the stone. Halathgar was there again, the same as in the entry chamber. The paint was bright blue this time, outlined in white.

Gil stepped ahead and wiped the dust off the image. The constellation shone brightly, and he did not even have to reach out with his mind to sense the lòhrengai about them.

"Here it is," he said. "Surely there is a room on the other side of these marks."

They paused. "What do you think it is?" she asked.

"I don't know. Perhaps a storeroom full of gold and treasure?"

"Maybe," she said. "Or perhaps a chamber where she worked her magic in secret."

That was possible too. But he felt that her magic, at least her great spells at any rate, were worked from the tower in which her tomb was eventually built.

He shrugged. There was only one way to find out. "Shall we?" he asked.

She nodded.

Gil put his hands to the constellation. The marks on his palms tingled. With a click and a rush of power, the door that he knew was there slid open.

They looked inside the next room. It was lavish, but still a small chamber – long but narrow. A couch, lush and soft, filled most of it. Dust covered it now, yet still the color of the fabric shone through. Royal blue.

The hangings on the wall were the same color. These were mostly intact, and they showed scenes of Cardoroth's history, and of the time even before the city was founded. Gil recognized images of the Camar race, his ancestors, camped in tents and villages by a great river. Beyond was a forest and within that a mighty city. That was Halathar, the home of the immortals who had befriended and taught many tribes of men. To them the various races of men owed much. But they had given much also of themselves in service, in war and battle against the enemies of the Halathrin before they ventured further east to found cities such as Cardoroth.

There were other images too. One showed the fabled standing stones, a place of worship and ceremony that dated back to his earliest ancestors. It was a place from history that was not forgotten, but that had become legend. It was from a time that Gil's books called the *Age of Heroes*.

He looked around at the tapestries. There were other stories on the wall, drawn from the ancient past. The migration of all the Camar tribes was there, ever travelling from west to the east. But there was war also. Great battles against the enemies from the south were shown. There were elugs, that race of creatures like men, which some knew as goblins, and their hordes blackened the wall-hangings. Elùgroths led them, cloaked in shadow and pointing wych-wood staffs with the menace of sorcery.

And then other tapestries showed Cardoroth: red-walled, splendid, its wide and myriad streets filled with joyous people – among them Carnhaina herself. Suddenly the image of her filled Gil's vision: a great lady, holding in one hand a spear while the other was raised, palm down, in a gesture of benevolence. About her neck was a torc of gold, an ancient symbol of nobility and rule.

Gil took his eyes off her. There were other things in the room also, although they seemed matter-of-fact by comparison. The desk and chair drew his gaze more than anything, and he realized that this was a secret room for Carnhaina. She had sat on that very chair, placed her hands on that very desk, lit or extinguished the lamp that still rested upon it.

At that moment, he felt a sudden connection to her. She was not just an ethereal spirit, not just a presence in his dreams. She had been, once, a living and breathing person with dreams of her own. She was his grandmother, many times removed.

On the desk was a book, but there were many, many others in shelves along the back wall. This was a library, or a study, and he felt beyond doubt that it was hers. It was a place she came for solitude, away from her court and the incessant demands of leadership. Here, she pondered things and then issued commands. This was perhaps the heart of her realm rather than the throne room.

He glanced at Elrika, but she said nothing. This was not a time nor a place for speech. He moved to the table and glanced at the book upon it. It was open. It was, perhaps, the last book she was reading before she died, and it had been left thus, undisturbed, through the long centuries. Yet if so, strangely, it had not accumulated much dust. Nor had the top of the table.

With trembling hands, he reached out and picked up the book. It was heavy. Turning it over he studied the script. It was written in a fine but spidery hand. The language was old, but still readable. The speech of Cardoroth had not altered much in the centuries, and Gil had read other books nearly as old as this.

The book had been left open on the table, spine up, but he saw at once that it had been left on the first page. Glancing at its top he saw something that made him gasp. There, in that spidery writing, there, written almost certainly by Carnhaina, was his own name. *Gilcarist*.

It was like a blow to his stomach that took his breath away. He realized that he was looking at a letter. It was

126

addressed to him, written by a person who had died nearly a millennium before his birth.

Elrika had seen it also. She backed a little away from him.

"Read it," she said. "It's for you."

Gil hesitated. It *was* for him, though how that could possibly be he did not know. What power of foresight had Carnhaina possessed? How great her skill in magic must have been? Yet still, he would not have been here without Elrika. So, he read the letter aloud.

"Hail, Gilcarist. Prince now, and mayhap king to be. When you read this, I am dead. Long years have passed. But know, though death has turned me to dust, still I have power. In death shall I guard my people even as in life I led them.

"One day, their governance may fall to you. But that is undecided, and even my arts have limits. I cannot see with certainty, and fate, as ever, is fickle. But long I knew you would come. By the time you read this, long will I have waited. For understand! Your coming is told in the stars. You are the Star-marked One. You are The Boy with Two Fates. The Guarded and the Hunted. The King Who Might Rule, or the Lòhren Who Might Teach. You are also the Boy Who Might Live, and the Boy Who Might Die. You are the Savior and the Destroyer. But to me, your foremother, you are my grandchild. You are Gilcarist, and I love you.

"Know, Gilcarist, that it is in your power to shape the destiny of your people. Know also that nothing is as it seems. Friends may be enemies, enemies friends. Or not. Trust few, but trust fully. Choose your companions wisely, for they will stand by you when the forces of the Dark seek your destruction. And they will. Remember that.

"We have met, or we will meet, or we will meet again. Until then, fare thee well. And know, O child, that in life I was stern. Even with my children. But I was proud of them, and I am proud of you. Good luck. You will need it, for the Dark conspires against you. Do not forget."

The letter ended. Gil ceased speaking. There was an immense hush in the room, and Elrika looked at him. There was awe in her eyes. Or perhaps fear.

12. Chaos Serves the Dark

The water of the lake calmed. The apparitions came to a standstill before her. They were near the shore, yet still above the water as though standing on a ledge of up thrust stone. But there was none.

Ginsar felt the cold of the earth burn her knees where she knelt, but she did not move. She had not the strength, nor the desire.

The taller of the two apparitions spoke, his voice a whisper of death in the frost-cold air.

"Why have you summoned me?"

"To learn, O Master."

"Then speak my name."

Ginsar knew this spirit's name, the name it bore in life. She knew also that to speak the name of a spirit was to give it greater power in the mortal world.

"Shurilgar," she answered without hesitation.

The shade drew itself up, Shurilgar that was, and the shadows that formed him took more substance.

"What would you know?" he asked.

"Will I succeed in contriving the downfall of Brand and the boy? Will I destroy them, and then kill them?"

Shurilgar stood like a ray of darkness spawned by a black moon. The shadows around his face were impenetrable. His voice, when he answered, seemed distant and empty as the void.

"I am no longer part of this battle. The dead have other concerns than the conflicts of this smallest of worlds." He paused. "Yet this much I will say. The fate of the boy remains undecided. The destiny of Brand is now set. He has made his choice, and he will now die. It is unalterable."

Ginsar cackled with glee. She knew better than to believe that Shurilgar was unconcerned with the outcome of her plotting, but his similitude of indifference did not matter. He played his own games, in death as in life, but none of that mattered. He had said that Brand would die, and the dead saw the future as the living could not.

She stifled her joy and looked back at the spirit. The long arm of Shurilgar, he who was and would always be her master, pointed slowly at her, and his voice was chill with anger.

"Beware! Brand's death is not an end. It is a beginning. If you be not careful, you shall snatch dry dust where you sought to scoop water."

The lake suddenly thrashed all about him, responsive to his mood. It hissed and spat. "Beware. Things are not as they seem. This much I am permitted to say, and no more. Beware!"

The lake stilled. Shurilgar drew in on himself. The shadows about him deepened.

"What else would you ask? Time grows short. Your summoning weakens."

Ginsar spoke quickly. "What of the city itself? It did not fall in the recent war, might it fall now, if Brand dies and the boy is friendless or dead also?"

Shurilgar replied, his voice remote and subdued. "You have brought forth the four riders. They are chaos. All now is possible. All. This may work to your favor. Chaos serves the Dark better than the Light. But beware. Not all ends can be seen, even by the dead. Chaos also serves the Light."

The dark spirit paused, lost in some recollection of the past or some glimpse of the future. "Remember that," he whispered. "But know also that the four riders, or the forces you have channeled into the bodies of those who once were men, call to others of the Dark. Your allies in the south were defeated. They will need time to recover, to grow again in strength. Your allies to the north gather. They shall flock to you, and an army you shall have."

Ginsar bared her teeth. "Then I shall conquer! With Brand dead, none will rally the city. None will have the strength to withstand me!"

The waters of the lake seethed and churned. They muttered angrily, impatient for release from the summoning that held them.

"Time is gone," Shurilgar said. His shadow form began to recede, gliding back toward the deeper water whence it had risen.

"Tell me!" Ginsar shouted over the growing distance and the splash and roil of the water. "Will I be queen of Cardoroth?"

Her master pointed at her once more, his long arm covered in the tattered shrouds of death.

"You shall triumph! Yet in the moment of your victory is the seed of failure. Beware!"

The dark form at her master's side cried out, just one voice now among the many that lifted up from the lake seeking life and freedom. But she *knew* his voice.

"Avenge me! Avenge me!"

Ginsar's blood burned with fire. "I shall, Felargin. I shall, my brother!"

The spirits sank beneath the waves. Her brother first and Shurilgar second, his long arm still pointing at her.

The lake swallowed them. It heaved and turned, and then grew slowly still. All noise ceased.

Ginsar staggered to her feet. Her strength was spent, yet a great joy bubbled within her. The dead did not lie. She would triumph! Yet still a single doubt nagged at her jubilance. What had Shurilgar meant by the seed of failure?

13. This is Home

"There's more," Elrika said. "Go on. Read some of it. It's for you."

Gil hesitated. The rest seemed to be a diary of some sort. It was too much to read at one sitting. Far too much, and it scared him. Yet it compelled him too. The words belonged to his far distant grandmother. They were written in her own hand...

He flicked through the book, noticing the spidery script alter from a firm and confident hand into a frailer one. Age and death had claimed her, despite her great power. Or perhaps she had let it do so, renouncing the longevity of lòhrens and sorcerers, not using magic to sustain her life as they did.

"There are dates at the top of each page," he said to Elrika. He did not tell her that the writing burned from the page into his eyes. Here were not just the thoughts of another person, but the history of another age. This was a kind of magic nothing to do with lòhrengai. It was a window through the wall of time and into another world.

One page caught his eye, and he read some of it out loud.

"I have it! Magic some call it. Lòhrengai. Sorcery. Witchery. What matter the name? It is the heart, body and mind of the user that gives it power and form. If these be unified, no spell is beyond reach, no power beyond summoning. When need is the greatest, do not let the unity slip away. Harden your will. Grasp it. Make the power your own, and then nothing is impossible."

Gil flicked to another page and read something new.

"Alas! Battle went against us this day. The Dark closed in. Hope was lost. All my power was as nothing. My armies were scattered before the winds of fate, and the great dark fell before my eyes. Yet one man saved us. A peasant. He withstood the rush – rallied his friends about him and the army after. Thus the battle turned. I do not even know his name, but today he was king."

The diary said nothing more of the conflict than that. Gil wondered what battle was being fought and what man had saved the day. But whatever had happened, and to whomever … they were all dead now, their life-and-death struggles forgotten. It was a lesson to him, a reminder of mortality and that the passage of time would one day expunge all memory of him, too. But for a little while, he had a voice, and he would make sure the world heard it. He had things to say, and to do, before he was swept into oblivion.

Elrika caught his glance. "Maybe we should go back now," she said. "You've been gone a long time, and the Durlin will be looking for you."

Gil drew himself out of his reverie. "You're right. But we'll come back."

He took a long look around the room. Apart from the diary, there were shelves of unread books. This was his place. This was his home. This was where he would discover, or decide, just who he was.

14. The Gaze that Misses Nothing

Elrika moved toward the door that they had used to enter the chamber.

"Wait," Gil said. He stood where he was, reasoning something through. "This room," he told her, "must have been Carnhaina's study, her secret library. At least while she was in the palace rather than her tower. She would not have entered it from far below. The stairs were built as a means of escape or for secret meetings. For everyday use, she would have entered from somewhere at the top, from somewhere convenient to her personal rooms."

"What are you getting at?"

"I think there's another way out, or into, this room."

They looked about, but there were no more eyes, no more images of Halathgar.

Gil felt defeated. He knew his reasoning was sound, but reality had proven it wrong anyway. He was about to give up, and then something occurred to him.

"She was a lòhren," he said, "Or a sorceress. But the top rooms of the palace are well frequented. Some sort of hidden mechanism would have been used, as with the other doors. But it would be constructed of magic so that it could not be accidently discovered. And the risk was greater up here, up where her rooms were because that's where people would have expected to find such a thing."

"But if it's not marked," Elrika said, "and if you don't know the spell, then how can you find or open it?"

Gil looked at the books on the shelves. It was possible that the answer might be written in there somewhere, but there was no time to look for it. Nor, he supposed, was it likely that Carnhaina would have written such a thing down. So, reasoning it through, it would therefore more than likely have been something easy to recall, something familiar and every day to her, but something unseen to anyone else.

And then he knew. The other doors had been marked with a sign and opened at the touch of his lòhrengai, but that was not the only way to construct a spell.

"Halathgar," he said in a solemn voice. It was still Carnhaina's mark, but spoken rather than painted.

Nothing happened. "Halathgar!" he said again, with more force. Still, nothing happened.

What was he missing? The word alone was obviously not enough – he would need to invoke lòhrengai with it.

He closed his eyes and slowed his breathing, thinking of Brand's oft-repeated advice. *Let the magic come of its own, rather than try to bend it to your will.*

Light glimmered on his palms. He tried not to think too deeply about it, but just accepted that it had come at his need. He faced the wall opposite, and reaching forth he placed his hand on the stone. "Halathgar!" he commanded.

Light flared, a brilliant blue that filled the chamber. He felt a power respond to his own. It rose up, sought him out, assessed him and then withdrew. And then suddenly there was a grinding of stone and another door appeared.

Gil dropped his hands and the light faded. Together, he and Elrika walked through the door. The room beyond was a surprise. It was Brand's own bed chamber. Once, it had been the king's, and Gil supposed it had always been so through the ages. Once, even Carnhaina had slept here.

There was no one about. The room was plush, even luxurious. It was so different from the way Brand normally was.

"Halathgar," Gil said, almost casually, and the door closed behind them.

They opened the door out, just an ordinary door this time, and a palace corridor was beyond. There was no one here, either. The servants had already made the bed in Brand's chamber and must have cleaned the other rooms on this floor as well.

They closed the door behind them and then hastened along the corridor. But almost straight away they heard someone walking, and then Brand himself turned a corner to face them. His expression seemed troubled, but instantly that look was gone, and then he held them both with his clear-eyed gaze that missed nothing.

"What have you two been doing?"

"Nothing!" they answered in unison.

Brand looked at them, a slight smile on his lips. Then it was gone, and Gil was not sure that it had ever been there at all.

"Shorty is looking for you. He's not happy that you gave his men the slip – again."

"I'm sorry," Gil said. He looked down at the floor.

"Don't apologize to me. Shorty is the one who deserves it. Or better still, the Durlin who were guarding you at the time that you … disappeared."

"I'll find Shorty right now, and then the guards," Gil said. He was surprised at how calmly Brand was taking this, and there was no suggestion of punishment. With

137

Elrika close by his side, he began to walk away, but Brand called after them and they turned.

"So," he said. "You found it." This time he did not hide his smile.

Gil was shocked, but he should have known that Brand would have found the chamber himself. He was a lòhren, not just the regent.

"Yes. But how did you know that?"

Brand's smile broadened. "Look at your boots. They didn't get like that walking around the palace. Not through the normal corridors, anyway." And then he turned and was gone.

Gil slowly shook his head. "Nothing escapes him."

Elrika did not answer at first. She remained staring down the empty corridor in awe.

"He's a great man," she said softly. "I don't care what they say. He'll never betray you."

Gil looked at her in surprise. "But he didn't even say hello to you. How can you know something like that?"

She shrugged. "He didn't speak to me, but he looked into my eyes, and I looked back. Trust me Gil, whatever is going on he is the person to trust most in all the world."

15. Speak My Name, Boy

Gil dreamed again that night, but he knew straightaway that it was not the normal dream.

He stood upon a knoll, looking down over sweeps of green grass. A gusty wind blew hard from the west, and the scent of rain was in the air. Clouds reached out across the sky, shifting, changing, growing and disappearing under ever-altering buffets of air. The sun winked and shone from behind the gray clouds, covered at times while at others breaking forth with piercing rays.

He stood alone in a great wilderness, but he was not scared. Dusk settled about him, and he knew that between blinks of his eyes hours had passed, as was the way with dreams.

The wind died down, and night drew over the land. The clouds blew away, and stars sprang to life. Out of nowhere a campfire burned before him. It flickered comfortingly.

Gil looked out beyond the fire, and by the light of stars he saw what he had not seen before: a forest. A great sweep of trees, dark and brooding, marched along the horizon. They were pines. They were just like the trees that surrounded Lake Alithorin. The forest even had the same feel to it. And then he knew. It *was* the same forest.

Gil sat down near the fire and thought. Somehow, he had been caught out of time. He was on a grassy knoll where the city of Cardoroth would one day be founded, near a thousand years before he was born. The idea of it made his mind spin. It was also possible, he supposed, that he was in the future, at a point in time so far ahead that the city was gone and no trace of it remained. *Nothing*. Yet he trusted his first instinct better. He was in the past; that was how it felt.

He looked now into the fire, and it drew him in deep. Tongues of flame turned and twisted, and the hot air trembled. There was an image within all the movement, vague and shimmery. Then a voice, born on hot air and wisps of smoke, came to him.

"Do not be frightened," it whispered. The words twisted through the air like the tongues of flame.

"I'm not," he replied.

A swift laugh came in answer, carried on a flurry of ember-sparks and swirling smoke.

The voice spoke again, suddenly warm and rich. "Speak my name, boy. And I will come to you."

Gil knew who it was. Cardoroth called her the Forgotten Queen. Some named her the Witch Queen. But neither was her name.

"You are Carnhaina."

The fire flared. Sparks flew. In a billow of smoke the image gathered form and stepped out of the flame. A woman now stood before him, tall and majestic. She gazed down upon him, her eyes still sparking with the light of flame. But the flame was blue, and it burned with a cold light. Her red hair spilled like blood over her pale skin, and both hair and skin were brighter than he remembered. Nor was she the large woman that he had seen atop the tower. Here, youth flushed her features and there was a twinkle of merriment in her eyes. Yet still the same gold torc gleamed about her pale-skinned neck, and as always, in her right hand she grasped an iron-headed spear. But he knew it was more than that. It was a lòhren-staff, and the power of magic played like running fire the length of its metal tip.

She smiled. "Only when you speak my name do I have the power to come. In the flesh."

He looked at her anew, and realized that she was as real as him, whatever that meant in a dream.

"Why have you come? Why am I here?"

"So many questions?"

He grinned back at her. "That's what Brand says. He also says that if you don't ask you don't get, and if you don't question you don't learn."

"A wise man is Brand. Wiser far than his years, for he is still young."

Gil stood up and bowed. When he straightened, he asked a very direct question.

"Will he betray me?"

"Do you think he will?" she replied immediately.

"Do you always answer a question with another question?"

He thought for a moment that he had overstepped the mark, but Carnhaina merely laughed.

"You have spirit, boy! Not many dare to banter thus with the dead."

He did not know what to say to that, and there was a momentary silence.

Carnhaina's mood changed. "This much I'll say, as I said once before. There is great danger. To you. To Cardoroth, and to Brand most of all. To save himself, he must lose."

Gil held her gaze. "That makes no sense."

"Ha! Mayhap it will in time. We shall see."

She pulled her mantle about herself, feeling a cold breeze that he did not.

"Sit," she said, and pointed with her spear to the grass. He did so, and to his surprise she sat down lithely and faced him.

They talked for a while, as grandmother to grandson. No longer was she a queen. She was proud of her line, she said. Proud most of all of Gil's grandfather. "But Gil," she said, "You may yet rise above them all. Cardoroth needs you, but before that … Brand will need you first."

"How so? I don't think he needs the help of anyone."

"Oh, you are wrong there. Brand is strong, but he will need to be. Few men have ever passed through such testings as has he in his life, and the testing has only begun. Even the strongest metal can shatter. Indeed, it *will* shatter if enough force is applied. And Brand is a man. That makes him both weaker and stronger, for while the *body* has limits, the *will* can endure beyond the constraints of the physical. Let us hope Brand proves that true."

Gil did not answer, and Carnhaina sighed. "You will understand better one day. For now, it is enough that you know how to get help when he needs it most."

"And how shall I know when he needs it most? And how shall I get it?"

"Hush, child. You will know. Oh, when Brand needs help, if things come to pass as I fear, and as I hope, then you will *know*. The how is much easier. I shall give you the means to summon me. But it will work once, and once only. Use it wisely."

She reached forth with her hand and traced her fingers along his temple. He felt the cold brush of death, of a void beyond the life he knew, dark and distant. But her touch seemed real also, born of flesh and blood. And there was

142

love in it. Then he felt her palm press against his skin. Something passed from her to him, but he could not grasp what it was.

She leaned back wearily, and dropped her hand. "It is done," she said. "When the time comes, you will know what to do and have the power for it. In the meantime, have courage. Endure. Never give up hope."

She said the last with a keen look in her eye. A while she looked at him thus, and then, almost regretfully, she raised her hand again, fingers thrusting toward him.

"Sleep," she said.

Gil tried to keep his eyes open, but he could not. Weariness stole over him. The night and the fire faded. Last of all disappeared Carnhaina, her eyes gleaming like the twin stars of Halathgar, and then they too blinked out. As he drifted into sleep her whisper followed him. *Sleep. Sleep, and have courage.*

16. I Rule!

Brand sat on the lesser chair beside the throne of Cardoroth. That ornate symbol, carved of ancient wood, embossed with gold script, crusted with gems, dominated the room. He ignored it.

It was morning. The early light of the sun beamed through the stained glass windows. The white marble of the floor glittered with light like the surface of a lake. Above, the vaulted ceiling rose to a dizzying height, grand and eloquent. It was all beautiful, but it did not take his mind off the troubles he faced.

A score of soldiers flanked him, standing poised and alert. Taingern and Shorty were among them. A soldier, ceremonially dressed, opened the great door to the throne room, and the delegation that had insisted on seeing Brand this morning came through. They did not look at the art of the grand room. They did not speak to each other. A dozen strong, grim faced, they strode purposefully toward him.

Brand knew these men, or some of them. The others, he knew of. Sandy had seen to that, and she was about somewhere, concealed in an alcove listening. Of that he was sure.

He knew what they would say. Sandy had told him, for there were few secrets in the city that she did not uncover. Few secrets, and few conspiracies. These men were aristocrats all, and even without her earlier warning he could have guessed their intentions. But it was nice to be forewarned anyway.

Their leader stepped to the front when they came to a stop. He did not bow.

"Do you know me, Brand?"

There was silence. Only the nervous shuffles of the soldiers broke it, and the faint clink of chainmail armor that they wore.

Brand ignored the lack of protocol at being addressed merely by name. He ignored the rudeness, and he allowed a faint smile to play across his face.

"I know you. You are Lord Dernbrael. Once, you commanded the right flank of Cardoroth's army when we fought enemies from the south. I know you, and your history. It's said that you are in league with the old king's half-brother, who has long sought to return from exile and claim the throne. Of course, that's only a preposterous rumor, and I don't believe it. This much I know, for I observed it first hand on that battlefield. You are a brave leader, for I saw you command with unflinching courage. I saw and watched while you stood on the hill and gave orders to your men who fought."

Dernbrael looked at him. There was puzzlement on his face as he tried to discern the meaning of what had been said to him. That puzzlement fled, and his face went red as he realized that he had been insulted twice under the guise of two compliments.

"The past is of no matter," Dernbrael said. "I come to speak of the future, and I will be heard."

Brand looked to the floor, as though in thought. "The death rattle of a thousand throats is what I hear. The cries of the dying, the shouts of the living and the roar of battle. I remember that still, hear it waking or sleeping. And I can picture you in my mind, a glorious figure on the hill, your cloak billowing out behind you, your sword, sheathed at your side … your pale armor glinting, free of dirt and

145

blood. Yes, Dernbrael, I know you. Your bravery earns you many rights. So speak. Speak, and be heard."

The soldiers stilled. Shorty and Taingern stiffened. Those two had been there that day, had fought in that same battle. They knew Brand had just called the man who stood before him a coward. They knew also the insult had been delivered as a calculated retribution for the lord's failure to meet protocol. What would happen next, nobody knew.

There was silence, deep and unbroken. Not even the great vaulted ceiling of the throne room cast back any whisper of sound, as it usually did.

Suddenly, Dernbrael laughed. "Thus do you offer me a reprimand for my own lack of courtesy. A wild man of the Duthenor some call you, but I perceive that you have a nimble mind and have learned refinement at our court. It is a place where words are edged like swords."

"So it is. And words can cut, but never yet have I seen them spill the guts of a soldier standing beside me, trying to hold the line."

Dernbrael looked at him coldly. "Are we done sparring?"

"Speak," Brand said. "And I will listen."

"Then this is what we have come to say." Dernbrael gestured at the nobles behind him. "You know it already, but let us clear the air. "Your rule is wrong. You are not one of us, not of Cardoroth. You do not understand, even after the years you have spent among us, our ways. And why should you? There is great history among the city's people, great traditions. You make decisions without thought of that, and it disturbs the people. There is unrest. If you were wise, you would go now while you have the thanks of Cardoroth's citizens. Leave it too late, and you will earn their enmity instead. Be wise, Brand. I urge you, be wise."

Brand leaned back into his chair. It was hard and uncomfortable. Momentarily, he glanced at the cushioned seat of the throne.

"Traditions, you say," he responded. "Traditions such as those that surround the position of Swordmaster. The Swordmaster that I dismissed. Perhaps I should have let him stay. After all, he was the son of the *last* Swordmaster appointed by the king. That is the sort of thing you mean, is it not?"

Dernbrael gave a curt nod. "That is exactly the sort of thing that I mean."

Brand rested his hands on the arms of the chair. "I see. A tradition had been established. It was not the place of an outsider to break it." Brand looked thoughtful, and then crossed his arms. "But does competence not mean anything? The man called himself a Swordmaster, but there are a hundred soldiers in the palace at this very moment who could best him with a blade. He was no Swordmaster. Worse, he was a fool. I dismissed him because he was not fit for the job, no matter who his father was, or who else he is related to. As it happens, I know he is your cousin. But you are as great a fool as he if you think that I will promote the aristocracy, or preserve their titles and duties, if there are others of less noble birth but greater ability to carry out those tasks. And you are a fool twice over if you think I will walk away from the regency. The king appointed me, and here I will stay until Gilcarist is ready to ascend the throne."

Dernbrael stiffened. "You dare call me a fool? The old king was the fool, appointing you! Old, did I say? Rather, I meant *senile*. Thus runs the whisper through the city. He was decrepit, and you are a mistake of his dotage. The people begin to see it. They begin to see your true purpose and goal, and they will have none of it!"

Brand felt a white-hot anger well up inside him. The old king had been his friend, and he deserved a better remembrance than this.

He stood from his chair in one smooth motion, and his hand rested on the hilt of his Halathrin-wrought blade. It was time to show them his anger.

"The king was a better man by far than any of you. By his wit, and by his courage and determination, he saved this city from destruction several times. Many are our enemies. They are in the north and in the south. Better might it have been if he had failed, and the hosts of our opponents had poured in to overrun the city. Then, I would not have to deal with the likes of you!"

The nobles gathered before him grew pale. Some fidgeted. But Dernbrael was not put off.

"These are our demands," he said coolly. "Too long you promoted commoners above the nobility. The nobility will negotiate amongst themselves who is best to take the throne. That may take a while, but it will not be the boy; he is too young. As you say, Cardoroth has many enemies. We can ill-afford either a boy or a foreigner to rule. Until a king is chosen, I shall act as regent." Dernbrael took a step closer. He was not armed, but he showed no fear at coming within reach of Brand's own sword. "This you will do, or there will be civil war. Think not that it is only the nobles gathered before you who rebel. All of Cardoroth is against you."

Brand sat back in his chair and thought quickly. When he spoke, it was almost to himself. "All this because I promote commoners?" He let out a long sigh. "Bah. Commoners are many, and the nobility are few. Why should it surprise you that they get promoted?"

Dernbrael considered that, and Brand smiled inwardly. The man was a fool, and Brand now had time to think

148

when instead he should have been backed into a corner and forced to make decisions quickly.

"It is not about numbers," Dernbrael said. "It is about rights, ancient rights and traditions."

"What you mean is that the nobility are born to rule, and the commoners are not."

Dernbrael lifted up his hands. "Such is life."

"Rubbish," Brand answered. "That's a pile of horse manure, and you know it." He stood up again. "You're so bent, Dernbrael, that I bet you can't even lie straight in bed at night."

Brand allowed himself another smile. He had had the time he needed to think. Now, he was deliberately speaking like a commoner in order to upset his enemy. Dernbrael would not like it. It would annoy him and the sudden change of tone would throw him off balance.

Brand pointed at him. "You would have the throne yourself, that much is obvious. And no doubt the nobility hate me, and plot against me. But just now you have committed treason. It was a mistake."

Dernbrael laughed. "Idiot. That alone should tell you that the power is mine, else I would not have dared it. If you leave now, you may leave with your life. If you stay, we will call a council of the nobility. It is in our power to do so. There is no doubt that the council will revoke your regency, and one of us will take your place. This is within the law."

Brand had reached the end of his patience, but he had thought things through and knew he was right.

"Maybe the council has the right to do that, and maybe they even would. Or maybe they wouldn't. The lawyers could debate it all for months, and the nobility may not see fit to place you on the throne, at any rate. But you're forgetting something."

Dernbrael smiled smugly. "I doubt it. But *do* tell."

Brand slowly drew his sword. "You call me a wild Duthenor, a tribesman, unfit to rule. Let me tell you then how a wild Duthenor tribesman thinks. I could kill you all now. Every one of you, and spill your blood in the throne room."

They shrank back. Even Dernbrael stepped away from him.

"Nothing could stop me," Brand continued, "for there is not a man among you. You speak of law? Then know this! Should I choose, I could rule by the power of the sword. The army is mine. I was one of them, remember? I shed my blood with them, as you never have, and they know it. Lawyers and councilors be dammed! The king made me regent, and regent I will be! Your demands are worth less to me than the dirt on your boots. Now leave, or you'll be taken out of here by bucket and mop. Have your council if you wish. It is nothing to me but leaves on the wind. I rule! And you cannot change it."

Even Shorty and Taingern went white at those words. The nobility stared at him, fearful that he would carry out his threat. But Dernbrael merely chuckled.

"Well. Then the rumor is true. I see it now. You would usurp the throne and set aside Gilcarist yourself."

Brand looked at him coldly. He sheathed his sword. "You know I could do so any time I want. But I haven't. Nor will I. Gilcarist will rule. He nears manhood now, and he learns well. He will take his place soon, and I will be free of the likes of you."

"So you say, but—"

"Enough! You are dismissed. You and your ragtag followers."

The nobles looked at him silently, and Dernbrael hesitated. But before any more words were spoken a soldier hastened through the room, his running steps loud on the marble floor and the echo of his coming thrown back down from the vaulted ceiling.

The room fell silent. The soldier came before Brand, short of breath and trembling.

My Lord," he said. "Three Durlin are slain. Gilcarist is missing."

The man did not speak quietly. All the nobles heard, and Dernbrael spoke into the silence that followed.

"So it begins."

17. Dark Rumors

Gil woke, and the memory of his dream, if dream it was, remained strong in his mind.

He felt a great sense of peace and belonging. But almost immediately those feelings, strong as they were, began to fade. Increasingly, he sensed that something was wrong. What had woken him? Had there been a noise?

He lay in bed, alert but still. He listened intently, but there was nothing out of place. Nevertheless, panic gripped him. There was no name for it. There was only a growing dread, without source or focus. But it was there.

He got up and dressed. Quickly, he belted a sword to his side. He did all this, his hands shaking badly, but there was still nothing out of place.

It was then that he heard a bump on the other side of his door. He stood motionless, his head cocked to the side, listening for more. A moment later the door burst open, torn off its hinges, and crimson fire flared within the opening and then winked out.

Three dark-cloaked figures rushed into the room. The light of dawn lit Gil's window, but these men from the corridor outside brought only darkness with them.

They came toward him. None of them carried a staff, but he knew they were elùgroths. Black-cloaked, their faces hidden by deep cowls and the skin of their hands pallid even in the dim light, they could be nothing else.

Gil tried to draw his sword, but he did not manage to free it completely from its sheath before a vice-like grip from one of those pallid hands clamped about his wrist. And then there were other hands grasping him and a fist smashing into his face. His head rocked back and pain flooded through him.

He struggled, but they were too many and too strong for him. They ripped the sword from his hand and discarded it on the floor. A knife was put to his back, and a face thrust up close before his eyes.

"Choose," an elùgroth said. "Live or die. Fight any more and your corpse will be left in this room."

Gil knew the man meant it. He went still, and he guessed this much at least; they were not assassins, else he would already be dead. They wanted him alive, and that gave him hope, though not much.

They moved out through the smoldering doorway. It was still quiet in the corridor, for likely the occupants of the rooms had been asleep, including the Durlin not set at guard at his door. It may be that they still slept, notwithstanding the noise.

The elùgroths hastened Gil forward, and then he saw the Durlin stationed outside his bedroom. All three were dead, strangled and burned by sorcery. The elùgroth who held a knife at his back made a gesture. The others worked quickly, dragging the bodies back into Gil's room. But there was another figure on the floor as well. It was an elùgroth, and Gil realized that the Durlin, though obviously taken by surprise, had still managed to fight back.

They closed the door and went forward. Another figure came into view, leaning against the wall. There was blood on his hand where he clamped it to his side. He too had been wounded by the Durlin, though not killed. Nevertheless, he looked badly injured. He muttered under his breath in some harsh language that Gil had never heard before, and straightened as they approached, ready to join them.

Gil understood. The elùgroth had been releasing a sorcerous spell. The air stank of it, and it was no doubt intended to ensure the occupants of the adjacent rooms slept deeply. He was sure that it was this that had woken him, but he was keenly sensitive to the use of magic through his training. The others did not have that benefit.

It might be a long time before this attack was discovered, and Gil considered crying out for help. But the knife hovered at his back, and he knew these men would kill him and flee if they had to, even if that was not their purpose.

The palace was in shadow and darkness, and like shadows themselves they flitted through the corridors. The sorcerer who cast the spell stumbled ahead of them, but he continued to chant and Gil felt drowsiness steal over him. He fought it off, but when he was alert again they were already in the palace stables.

He drifted once more, but knew that he had been seated on a horse. The elùgroth rode behind him, one hand on the reins and the other with a knife still at his back.

Through the streets they raced in mad flight. But they were not elùgroths with him anymore. Now they were soldiers of Cardoroth, or so they seemed. Gil could not focus on them clearly.

The sun came up. Light glittered. It dazzled his eyes, and he realized that he was out of the city, come through the gate and that a road lay before him. Beyond, the western horizon was green.

He guessed where they were going. That strip of green was the pine forest that surrounded Lake Alithorin. He had heard dark rumors of that place. It was legendary, woven through the folklore of the city and bound with a heavy history of evil. Shadowy things dwelt there, neither man nor beast. Magic lurked beneath the trees, magic and death for the unwary. It was forbidden to him, but now he did not doubt that he would learn some of its secrets. But what then?

The elùgroths, if elùgroths they were, held him prisoner. But they were servants of someone else. For whom did they act? Were outside forces trying, as ever, to bring Cardoroth down? Or did his captors owe alliance to some traitor within the city?

The last thought disturbed Gil most of all. How had these men known which room he slept in? How had they navigated the palace so swiftly on their way out?

The sun rose higher. The horses sped beneath them. The elùgroth who had chanted in the city slumped on his mount's back. When at length he fell, the others did not slow. He was dead, or soon to be dead. The Durlin had claimed him, Gil thought with grim satisfaction. *Good for them.*

18. The King's Huntsman

Brand questioned the soldier who stood before him in the throne room.

"What's known so far?"

"Gilcarist is gone. His sword was found on the floor of his bedroom."

"And the Durlin?"

"Dead. They were in the room. And…" the man hesitated.

"Speak!" Brand said. "Speak freely but swiftly."

"It seemed as though sorcery was used. There were strangle-marks about their neck, but there were burns also. And the door was charred."

"Is there more?"

"There are reports of four strange men and a boy riding away from the palace. But they are unreliable."

"Why so?"

"Because some say they saw black-cloaked riders, others soldiers and some … Durlin, or at least riders in white surcoats."

There was a momentary silence. Not even Dernbrael spoke, but there was a sneer on his face.

"Which direction did the riders head toward?"

"On that, strangely, all witnesses agree. They went west."

Brand turned to Shorty and Taingern. "The enemy has him. They will have gone through the West Gate, the Arach Neben. The forest around Lake Alithorin is where they will head. Evil always finds a home there, and there we shall find Gil. This much at least I can say. He is not dead. Otherwise, his body would have been left in the room. This is no assassination, and other plots are afoot." He turned his gaze to Dernbrael.

"We will speak later, if chance allows. And remember, I'm not from Cardoroth, as you earlier reminded me. I'm a barbarian. Should I discover that you were involved with this in any way, your aristocratic blood will not save you."

Dernbrael shrugged, but did not answer. He left, taking his group of nobles with him. None of them bowed as they left, but Brand was already issuing orders.

"Send for the Durlin," he said to Taingern. "All of them, whether on duty or not. We'll gather at the palace stables."

Taingern left, and Brand turned to Shorty. "Find Hruilgar, and bring him to the stables also."

"The king's old huntsman?"

"Yes. He still lives in the palace. Find him and bring him. We'll need a tracker, and none is better than that old man."

"What of the army, Brand? If the prince is held hostage, shall we not need soldiers also?"

"No. This is not an enemy of opposing soldiers that we face, as Cardoroth often has before. This is different. This is an enemy of sorcery. Quickly now! Do as I say."

Shorty left, and Brand looked around him. The throne room was silent, but word would get out swiftly of what had happened. He wondered what the people of the city would make of all this. But it was not really hard to guess.

He looked at the soldiers still flanking him. Their eyes were upon him, filled with doubt. He considered that. These men were loyal to him, and the doubt in their eyes was not concern about his motives, but about the wisdom

157

of chasing after Gil with only the Durlin and the old tracker instead of the army. No matter. He knew what he was doing.

Quickly, he went to the stables, detouring only briefly to retrieve something from his room. It was a long object, bundled in cloth and tied with two thin straps of leather. Then he went down to the stables and found the Durlin gathering.

They saddled their horses, and Brand chose his old black stallion. It was a reminder of his past, a time when he was a stranger to this city. It seemed long ago now, and the world had changed since then. So had Cardoroth, and so had he. Nothing was the same. Nor would it ever be again.

Taingern came, and with him the last of the Durlin. Only Shorty was absent, and when he arrived they would be twenty-seven: three short of their true number of thirty. Three would never ride again.

Shorty came soon after. With him was an old man, white-haired and silver-bearded. His face was ruddy and wrinkled from long years in the sun. Brand looked at him, surprised at how old he seemed and doubtful that he could make the journey. It had been at least a year since they had last met, and Brand wondered if he had miscalculated.

But the old man mounted the horse prepared for him without difficulty and sat astride it with the look of someone at ease.

Brand nudged his horse over. "Hruilgar," he said as greeting.

"Brand," the other replied. He had never been much for formality, and Brand liked that about him.

"Shorty has told you what's happened?"

158

"Yes," the old man answered. It was another good sign. The man wasted no time on useless speech.

"I think they've taken Gil into the forest. Once through the Arach Neben, you'll take the lead." Brand paused. "I'll rely on you most of all. We can do nothing unless we find the boy."

"If there's a trail, I can follow it," Hruilgar said simply.

Brand waited no longer. "Men," he said to the Durlin. "This will be dangerous. But our honor as Durlin is at stake, and our honor as men. We will find Gil. We are sworn to protect him. We will not give up. Speed now is our friend, rather than numbers. But mark my words, there will be sorcery at the end of our ride. Stay clear of it. There will be death also."

He almost said more, but even as he uttered those last words they triggered a premonition. As surely as he could see the men before him, he also saw glimpses of what was to come. The magic was both curse and blessing. He did not know which it was just now, but swift as the second sight came, just as swiftly it left.

The Durlin drew their swords when he stopped speaking. Their white surcoats gleamed, and they shouted the Durlin creed:

Tum del conar – El dar tum!
Death or infamy – I choose death!

Without another word, Brand nudged his horse into a gallop and the others followed. Through the streets they raced, and the clatter of hooves on cobbles was loud. The citizens gave way, melting into alcoves and hugging the side of the road. Some cheered as they passed, and Brand knew that word of what had happened had already gotten out into the city. This was a dangerous thing, for rumor would spread with it, and, under the circumstances, rumor was not his friend. When he returned, if that would ever be, he might find the city turned against him. But if so, that was a problem for another day.

They rode ahead. The city was large, but they reached the Arach Neben swiftly and passed through the shadowy gate tunnel.

Brand shivered in the sunlight on the other side. This was where he had met the horseman. This was where he had met Death. And he knew now that he would meet him again.

He shrugged off the doubt that beset him and slowed down. There would be time now to spare the horses, for the old man would go at a slow pace to track. He must be careful not to miss any sign, especially if the riders they pursued left the road. Once they were in the forest, it would be slower still, but the tracking would be easier.

Hruilgar came to the fore. He led them now, his head low over his mount while his eyes scanned the ground.

Within moments the old man stopped. He pointed to the ground.

"Four riders," he said. "They passed this way not long ago. The one who leads them rides erratically. He is injured. See! One of the others carries a heavy burden, or two ride the same horse. Its tracks are deeper in the dirt."

"How fast do they ride?" Brand asked.

"Swiftly. The tracks are far apart. There is fear upon them. And well should there be – I have their trail now." The old man spat to the side of the road. "I'll not lose it. Not unless they use sorcery."

Hruilgar waited for no answer. He kicked his mount forward and the hunt began.

On they rode. The sun rose high in the sky and beat down. The red granite walls of Cardoroth grew smaller and smaller behind them. The green strip of forest ahead grew larger. Brand looked behind him. There were signs of old battle there. The wall was pock-marked from attacks. The ground was scarred by the encampment of a massive army. The enemy of the south had broken themselves on that wall. He remembered that army well. But this battle was different. He could not help but wonder if he would ever see those walls again. Or the green fields of the Duthenor that he yearned for.

There was no one else on the road. It was deserted, deserted and silent. The Durlin did not speak. Nor did Hruilgar, but it was clear that he followed the trail, and he did so with confidence. It surprised Brand when the tracker pulled his horse to a stop.

He nudged his mount forward and drew level with the old man.

"What is it?"

Hruilgar shifted uncomfortably in his saddle, and then lifted a thin arm to point ahead. He did not speak.

It took Brand a moment to realize what the tracker indicated, then he saw. There were crows ahead. Black dots from this far away, but he saw them hop and flutter on the ground. On the road. They had been attracted to something. And crows were carrion eaters.

He looked at the old man. The old man did not meet his gaze. They both knew that Gil could be out there.

"Be wary of a trap," he said to all the riders. He did not think there would be one, for he saw no obvious places for concealment. But the crows, and what they portended, might divert the Durlin's thoughts. He did not doubt the enemy might well look for such an opportunity.

161

The group cantered ahead. Dust rose from the sun-bleached road. Soon, the cawing of the crows grew loud. More flew in from the surrounding wild.

Something took shape on the road ahead. The crows tore and pecked at it. They fought and struggled amongst themselves. They paid no heed to the approaching riders.

Brand drew to a halt some thirty paces away. He studied the scene. A body lay there, bloating already in the sun. The crows tore at it. But it was muffled in dark clothes, and he could not tell if it was Gil. It could be an elùgroth. But if so, how? Had they fought among themselves?

He studied the surrounds. He saw no one else, no trap, nothing but the drying grass and the odd clump of trees. The old man pointed again, and Brand saw it. A lone horse standing beneath the shade of a distant tree. It had no rider, or none that was visible.

"First things first," Brand said without emotion. He nudged his horse forward toward the body. Shorty and Taingern came with him. The others held back.

The crows cawed madly and then fluttered away. Some flew and landed nearby. Others perched in the closest trees and watched with bloodied beaks and beady eyes.

Brand dismounted. The corpse lay face down, but a hand stretched out, clutched into a claw. It was a pallid hand, blue-veined and bony. It was the hand of an elùgroth, a sorcerer who lived by night rather than day, shunning the sun. Shorty and Taingern saw it also. Brand heard them both let out a sigh of relief.

"Why is there is no staff such as they usually carry?" Shorty asked.

"They relied more on stealth than sorcery," Brand answered. "But the lack of a staff does not mean that an elùgroth cannot conjure magic. They can, and they did."

He turned the corpse over with his boot. It was a middle-aged man, and one eye stared up at him. The other was a bloody socket. The crows had begun their work.

"Look," Shorty said. "There's blood."

Brand looked lower. Sure enough, the black cloak was caked with blood. Brand drew a knife and bent. He ripped at the material and exposed the flesh beneath. There was a wound there, small but deep. It had been a killing stroke by a long knife. But not immediately lethal.

"I think," Brand said, "that this was no fight amongst the elùgroths. The Durlin who guarded Gil fought. One elùgroth they killed on the spot, but this is a second. They did the best they could, even though they were outmatched."

He signaled Hruilgar to come over. If the old man was disturbed by the sight of death, he did not show it.

"Can you tell anything from the tracks?"

The old man rode slowly around the corpse, and then trotted ahead a little way before coming back.

"It's simple enough. The man fell from his saddle, and the others kept riding. They did not miss a stride."

Hruilgar spat again, his contempt for the riders obvious, but unspoken. "The man did not die straight away. He crawled for a little, perhaps tried to reach some shade, but he did not have the strength."

Brand stood. They had learned all they could here. The riderless horse might reveal more. He got on his own mount and they went back to the Durlin.

"Be wary," he said. "Keep your eyes open. The enemy hastens, and that means they fear us. As well they should.

163

But they may also seek to ambush us. First, we will get that horse, and then we will ride again."

He led them off the road and toward the horse that stood beneath the tree. Soon, they came to it, and it was clear that there was no trap. There was nothing there but the horse, the tree and withered grass.

Brand gave a sign and one of the Durlin went over. Carefully, he approached the horse, whispering to it soothingly and taking hold of the reins that trailed on the ground. It was nervous, but he did not have much trouble.

"Unsaddle it," Brand said. "Remove the bit and set it free."

The Durlin did so and was about to return.

"Look in the saddlebags, son," Hruilgar called out.

The Durlin bent over and rummaged through their contents.

"Nothing," he said.

"Nothing at all? Not even food?"

"No. Nothing."

Hruilgar turned to Brand. "That's good."

"How so?"

"Because tracking is more about getting into the mind of what you follow than studying the physical trail it leaves. That this sorcerer had no provisions means, likely enough, the others didn't either. That shows they did not intend to ride far, or that they would soon meet with others who waited for them."

Brand gave a slight nod. "The forest is their destination. And there *will* be others." He said no more. They turned back toward the road and made for it. He felt the eyes of the Durlin on him. They sensed that he knew more than he was saying. That was true, but he could not tell them. It would make no difference.

He closed his eyes momentarily against the harsh sun. But he did not see blackness. Instead, another vision of the future came. He rode beneath the shade of trees. A cave mouth opened ahead, and then he was inside. It was darker here. Cooler. Filled with a sense of doom. He recognized it; it was the feeling of death. It rose from the floor. It fell from the shadowy roof. It was in the very air he breathed. And it suffocated him.

He opened his eyes to the sun again, and shrugged off the vision. The second sight was not strong with him. It was not reliable. Other lòhrens were more gifted at it than he.

But he knew he was only trying to convince himself. The more he used the power, the more the visions came. But right or wrong, visions or no, he had a task to do and he would carry it out.

They took up the pursuit again a little way ahead of the dead elùgroth. The crumpled body receded behind them. The crows had gathered to feast again, and they paid the living riders no heed. Slowly, their croaks and caws faded into the distance.

Hruilgar was at the fore again. Brand wondered if they would need him after all. The elùgroths had made no attempt to hide their passing, nor would they once they reached the forest.

They *intended* for him to follow. He knew that now, knew it for certain.

The group had not gone more than three miles when the old man slowed and studied the ground carefully.

"Tracks," he said. "There are many now. A dozen or more riders met them here. They were waiting."

"Keep going," Brand said.

The old man gave him a strange look, but said nothing. The tracker did not like the feel of things. He was one to trust his instincts, and Brand could not fault him on that.

They moved forward slowly now. Hruilgar was careful to make sure those they pursued did not leave the road in the confusion of all the tracks. Brand said nothing. But he knew they would not.

At length, the road petered out to a dusty track. Ahead was the fringe of the great pine forest that surrounded Lake Alithorin. No one had ever explored it. Not properly. Few of those who tried ever returned to Cardoroth.

Brand looked back over the distance they had travelled while Hruilgar once more studied the tracks. Cardoroth was still visible, red and hulking on the horizon. It was not a pretty city, but it had become his home. The wild barbarian who had first seen it years ago had died. He was a different man now. And he knew that his life was about to change yet again.

"They went into the forest," Hruilgar said. "All of them."

"We will follow," Brand replied. "Take us to their lair."

Slowly, they moved into the trees. Once more he felt the eyes of the men on him. He had said little, and his mood was grim. It was not like him, even under circumstances such as these, and they knew it. They knew something was wrong, but they did not know what. Not for sure.

It was not only dark beneath the tree canopy, but cooler. And quieter. It was quiet as the tomb. But Brand had been here before. And Shorty also. They knew what to expect, and the Durlin were brave men, not easily scared by folklore and superstition. But they knew also that trouble lay at the end of this ride. They rode in silence, alert, watchful, ready.

They rode into thicker forest, following a wispy trail into the gloom. And the murk welcomed them. Brand's mood was one with it. It was a dark place, a fitting place for dark deeds.

19. We Are Strong!

Gil became more alert as the morning wore on. Whatever sorcery the elùgroths had used to lull him, they had ceased to employ. Or, it may be, that the only one of them who had that power was the one who had died on the road. Could he make use of that? Were the others unskilled at sorcery? If so, he may have a chance to escape.

Escape! How he longed to do that, but sorcery or otherwise there seemed little chance of it now. Near the forest other sorcerers had joined the group. They all watched him closely. They all looked at him with hidden knowledge in their eyes. They all knew what their destination was and the plan for him. He, on the other hand, knew nothing. Nothing except that the leader for whom they had done all this was a woman. They whispered her name, and he saw adoration mingled with fear on their faces when they did so. She possessed great power, even if they did not. And the more he studied them the more he came to believe that. They were elùgroths, but they were not of the same kind or stature as those who had threatened Cardoroth in the recent war.

The morning wore away and they rode, single file, toward the sweeping expanse of Lake Alithorin. They followed a path so faint that Gil doubted anyone would have found it but them. Yet, if anyone followed, if anyone knew to follow … or cared to do so … the trail was now beaten and marked by their passage.

The path snaked back and forth, not seeming to head anywhere in particular, but it always drew them deeper into tall stands of pine. It grew dark beneath the tree canopy, and the air was dank and acrid with the smell of decomposition. Bright orange fungi flowered in lush growths on fallen trunks and long lengths of gray-green moss trailed from overhead branches.

The elùgroths slowed and dismounted, walking their horses forward. Gil was pulled down and prodded ahead also. Travel was difficult with his hands tied behind his back and twisted roots beneath his boots.

Gil looked around as best he could while they progressed. It was a different world here, inside the forest. It was an unnerving place, but he could not quite put his finger on what disturbed him.

Eventually, the trail widened just a little and climbed uphill, away from the lake. Even during the day fog drifted from the water and cast seeking fingers through the trees. Moisture clung in a film over the pine leaves and dripped from their needle-like ends.

Soon, the forest thinned and they faced rugged cliffs. The jagged overhang of the crags ensured the crannied rock-face was obscured by shadow. The path came to an end, and the riders spread out over the short grass of a meadow.

One of the elùgroths grabbed Gil roughly by the back of the neck and pointed at the cliff.

"Behold! You see the home of our Mistress. It is a place of treasures beyond your imagination. The wealth of kingdoms and the luster of gold lie within. And power such as you have never seen!"

Gil scrutinized the cliff-face. After a few moments, he saw a cave; the entrance was little more than a man-sized shadow. He wondered how deep it went and what lay within, but he knew that he would find out soon enough.

Most of the elùgroths began to walk their mounts further along the meadow. Three stayed with Gil, giving their mounts to others to tend. These three led him up to the cliff-face and to the cave.

A musty smell came from the opening, but Gil could see nothing within. They moved into the cave, and one of the elùgroths retrieved a lantern from the floor and lit it. By its swinging light, Gil saw something of what lay ahead.

The entrance was small and confined, but the cave soon widened into a large chamber with a sandy floor. There were tracks in the sand showing the passage of many booted feet over a long period of time. The cave continued, but at a downward slope.

The elùgroths hastened Gil forward, and he soon noticed that the walls grew damp as they descended. Beyond doubt, they were already below the water level of the nearby lake, and were going deeper still. The floor eventually opened up into a pit. Light rose from within, and there was a murmur of voices also. They descended, following a crude ramp of gravel and rock.

They came to the bottom. The floor here was of dirt, and there were signs of mud all about, but it had dried into hard crusts on the lower portions of the walls, pale and flaky.

Gil noticed also that the walls were no longer natural. They were formed of chiseled stone. He did not doubt that the floor, had he been able to see it under the patchwork of sand and dried mud, would have been constructed of flagstones.

Glancing about he saw that the walls were decorated with the remnants of tapestries, long since rotted and spider-haunted. At some time in the past the chamber had been fashioned deep below the surface, and later destroyed by flood.

Who, Gil wondered, had built this place? But it was of no concern to him now. Ahead, was a series of statues. They almost seemed to move in the swinging light of the lantern. There were sculptures of men and women, the features of both stern and aloof. The men had the appearance of prideful warriors, and the women were beautiful but cold as the stone of which they were made.

Beyond the statues was a dais. Upon it a throne. This was of wood, black and polished. It must have been above the reach of the waters that flooded the chamber. It was intact, the arms and legs carved with ornate scrollwork.

Behind the throne was a wall, covered by a great tapestry, ancient but still beautiful. But it was she who sat upon the throne that Gil looked at, and could not take his gaze off.

It was her. The woman from his dreams. Beautiful she seemed, and terrible. Colder was her glance than the lifeless gaze of the statues. Cruelness etched her high-cheeked face and the red curve of her lips. Anticipation, burning, smoldering, barely held in check, leaped and danced in her eyes like a cold flame. About her, cowed by her, made insignificant by her presence, dozens of elùgroths stood: mute, silent, mere shadows of her power and glory, acolytes to her beauty and darkness.

Gil came to a trembling stop. An elùgroth at his side prodded him on; there was still some way to walk before he came directly before her. *Her.* His enemy, in dreams and now in waking life, for he sensed enmity roil from her in waves. She hated him with a consuming passion.

He tried to think clearly, but his thoughts were despairing. She had power greater than any he had ever sensed. It hit him like a slap across the face. If the magic gave Brand power like this, he veiled it. Slowly, he shuffled forward, and a chill filled his body, seeming to settle into his very bones. Think! What would Brand do?

But he knew that he did not have Brand's skill at combat, nor at magic. These opponents far outpowered him, even without *her.* So, then what? What could he do?

171

Nothing? No, Brand would not do that ... then what was left? Very little, but he would do it. He would engage his captors, extract what information he could, and then wait for any chance that might turn things in his favor.

"Who is she?" Gil whispered to the nearest elùgroth.

A mocking smile crossed the man's face. "You will see."

"Brand will come for me, you know."

The smile widened, but the elùgroth did not reply.

Gil did not like the feel of that answer. Did they know that Brand would come, because he was a part of this? Or did they set a trap for him, and hoped that he would spring it?

It was time for a different approach. "You're all elùgroths, aren't you?"

"Yes."

"But you're not like the ones I heard of or saw during the war."

"No!" the man whispered harshly. "They serve in their way, and we in ours. But we of the north are different. Sparse, but we are strong!"

"Who is your leader? Who is *she*?"

"One who knows you, but you don't know her. Now, be silent."

Gil did not ask any more. He shuffled slowly forward, thinking on what had been said, and if he had learned anything. This much he guessed, whoever these elùgroths were, and he did not think they were powerful, they were all here now in this chamber. But it was not them that he, or Cardoroth, really had to worry about. It was her.

The dais was surrounded by burning torches. Smoke scented the air and shifted and moved across the shadowy ceiling. Before the throne, set upon a black-clothed table, stood a silver basin. He knew its purpose. It was a vessel used to scry, and that was a difficult task. Great power was needed, but also dark rites. Brand had once told him with distaste how it worked. Lòhrens did not employ the practice, but relied on visions instead.

He braced himself and raised his eyes to look at the lady again. This time she was much closer. She was all that he had seen and sensed before, but he noticed one new thing. There was not only power, and coldness and cruelty in her gaze as she looked back at him, but also madness.

Gil felt scared all over again.

20. He Comes!

The dark lady looked into Gil's eyes. "Do you know who I am?"

Her voice was deep and resonant. It did not seem to fit her tall and slim body. He realized that she used elùgai to enhance it, and that gave him insight into her personality. For all her power, she felt the need to impress. In that way, if no other, she was weaker than Brand.

"No," he replied simply.

She seemed annoyed at his answer. "Then learn!" The lady smiled at him suddenly, shifting from thought to thought and mood to mood too swiftly for him to follow. It was another sign of her madness. Gil was sure of it.

"I am older than I look," she said. "Old as the hills I am. I was born before Cardoroth, hovel that it is, was raised from the dust, stone by red stone."

Gil watched her closely. She seemed to be speaking more to herself than him, and he did not believe her claim, but with lòhrengai and elùgai, all things were possible.

She leaned forward and whispered, as though telling a secret to him alone, oblivious to the elùgroths at her left and right.

"In those days that are forgotten, I had a master. I have him still, though he is dead. Do you know *his* name?"

Gil tried to remain calm. He did not know what to expect from her, still less did he have any idea what she was talking about.

"No, lady, I do not."

"Then I shall tell you. Step closer."

Gil did not wish to. Nor did the elùgroths by his side push him. Nevertheless, under her gaze, he stepped forward.

"Good boy," she said, looking at him knowingly. "Listen then. This is a name that all Alithoras knows. Mighty he was. Mightiest of them all, save one. *That* name we do not speak, but my master was … my master is … Shurilgar."

It was a name that Gil had indeed heard. It was a name from legend, a name of infamy. Shurilgar. Shurilgar the Betrayer of Nations. The sorcerer had died long ago, so long that history and myth had become one. The Age of Heroes his books called it. But for all that the elùgroth had lived so long ago, still the whispered stories came down through the ages. His name was a byword for treachery, dark deeds and sorcery. And it was rumored that his acolytes survived him.

The sorceress flashed him a sudden smile, all white teeth and red lips.

"Ha! I see you know *that* name, as well you should. Now, you will discover mine, and you will learn to hold it in dread even as you fear my master."

She drew herself up from the throne and stood. Regal she seemed, and power glittered in her eyes. Her glance was as a spear cast by a fierce warrior, sharp and piercing, and Gil flinched before it.

"Kneel, boy! For I am Ginsar, Mistress of Sorcery and Queen of Darkness. Kneel, for even Death rides at my whim and bows in my presence.

Gil felt his legs weaken. He did not kneel, rather he stumbled to his knees. He knew that she used sorcery to awe him, but he could not resist her.

175

Tall she was, a slender thing yet filled with the strength of unbreakable steel, and the light of the torches seemed to flicker as a crown atop her head. Yet the shadows about her feet deepened and swirled like drifts of smoke. She was queenly, otherworldly, a thing of terrible beauty.

Her acolytes moaned and prostrated themselves. And yet, as swift as she had called up her power, she let it go. Once more she seemed as a normal woman, save for the flicker of madness in her eyes. She sat down and grinned at him.

"What is my name, boy?"

Gil struggled to his feet. "I heard you. Your name is Ginsar."

She smiled at him sweetly. "That is my name. You will not forget it. Ever." Her gaze fell away from him and became vacant, as if she saw something that no one else in the room could observe. But then she focused on him again, her eyes boring into him. "I have a brother also. Once, Felargin and I served the master. Perhaps you have heard of him?"

Gil shook his head. "No," he answered, and fear tightened his throat and made his voice waver.

"No matter," she said. Then she giggled. "I'm more famous than he is."

A cold anger began to burn in Gil. This woman was mad. And she had great power. But he would not cower before her. He was the son of kings.

"I have never heard of him. Nor have I heard of you." He did not raise his voice, but he spoke with clarity and confidence.

Once again, Ginsar's mood changed rapidly.

"Fool!" she screamed at him. "I am told that you have some power. Can you not sense it in me? Can you not feel that I hold your life like a strand of spider's web in my fingers? Pah! You are descended from a second-rate sorceress."

Gil straightened and a calm stillness settled over him. What would be would be, but he would not accept insults in silence.

"Carnhaina was a lòhren," he said, "not a sorceress."

The elùgroth to his side struck him across the face, but he ignored that and returned Ginsar's gaze.

She shrugged nonchalantly. "Lòhren. Elùgroth. How little you understand. There is not much that separates us." She pointed a long arm at him. "But what of you? Is your magic of the Light or the Dark?"

Gil stared at her, taken by surprise, and he did not answer.

"Ha!" she said. "We shall see!"

Suddenly, he felt the full force of her mind. He realized in that moment how gentle Brand had always been with him in their training. Her power was overwhelming. It was like being crushed under a mountain. Slowly, surely, against his will he felt the magic inside of him being grasped and squeezed. She forced it out of him, made it gleam in the air between them, silver, blue and green. It was a shimmer of light, flickering colors as they each vied for control.

But she was mightier than he. His strength gave way before her. His will crumbled.

She reached into his mind and called forth an image. It was a memory of his grandfather, but she made it her own. The king of Cardoroth now stood between them. A crown was upon his head. He was old, his once-black hair turned silver with age, but leanness and strength were etched into his frame. He had something of the look of a wolf about him: patient, but fierce and bold when necessary. He shimmered with light, and then turned to smile at Gil. But it was his grandfather no more. Instead, the face shimmered and became Brand's. The crown flared with silvery light upon his head.

Tears streamed down Gil's face, but Brand gave him a mocking bow. He straightened, and uttered a single word. *Elùgrune.* And then the image stepped to the side so that Gil looked into Ginsar's eyes.

"Carnhaina was a fool," she said. "And your grandfather was a fool. So too is Brand. Only I have the true power. Nothing is beyond me."

Gil felt the cold anger inside him begin to burn. He would test her claim, if he could.

With a sudden determination, he wrenched control of the image from her. He made it turn, a blade appearing in its hand. It strode toward Ginsar, and surprise appeared on her face. But swift as that look came it left, and with a wave of her hand the image faded.

Gil staggered back, and Ginsar cackled. But he sensed that what he had done had startled her. She was not invulnerable. But then he remembered Death. It was not just she who was the enemy. It was also the powers she had loosed upon the world. Whatever weaknesses she had, she controlled forces beyond the strength of any man to fight.

Gil heaved for breath, exhausted by fear and drained by the use of lòhrengai. In the silence, an elùgroth scrambled down the ramp of ancient rubble and ran the length of the subterranean hall toward his mistress.

"He comes!" the elùgroth called, and there was fear in his voice. Hope rose in Gil. He knew who it was. Then he wondered if it was fear in the man's voice, or excitement.

Ginsar confirmed his growing suspicion. "Of course Brand comes. That is the plan, fool."

She turned her gaze back to Gil and smiled wickedly. "Do not take heart from this, boy. Brand brings someone with him. His name is Death."

21. Live, or Die

The elùgroths who ringed the dais stood still. Ginsar waited. She seemed calm and serene, but her breath came quick and her chest rose and fell rapidly.

Slowly, noise penetrated down to the chamber from the outside world, and a glimmer of light came with it. Then Gil saw them. There were Durlin, their white surcoats gleaming. Hruilgar was with them also. Of course, he was a tracker, and Brand would have needed him. But it was the man who came before them all who drew his eyes.

Brand led them. He came down the rocky slope of rubble, poised and balanced though loose stones and dirt shifted beneath his boots. To his side was sheathed the great sword that he had borne on many adventures. Gil had hefted that blade. He knew its history and its quality. And he knew the fighting skill of the man who carried it. There was none better.

In Brand's left hand was a long object, wrapped in cloth. Gil could not be sure what it was, but he guessed. His gaze shifted to the Durlin who filed down behind the regent. He regretted now that he felt stifled when they guarded him. He regretted that he had not understood them better. Now, he realized they could die if they tried to save him, just as had the three who had stood watch before his door in the palace.

Yet, he soon came to see that there were only the Durlin, and there was no sign of soldiers from Cardoroth. Why was that?

There was no sound but the rasp of boots on stone as Brand and his men walked down the long aisle of statues toward the dais.

The Durlin held their hands on the hilts of their swords, but they did not draw steel even though they now approached the elùgroths.

Brand, at their head, still held the cloth-bound object, but his right hand hung easily by his side. There was no emotion on his face. His features were the perfect mask of lòhren inscrutability. He never faltered in his step, either coming down the treacherous slope or walking the shadow-haunted hall between the statues. He seemed sure-footed and unconcerned by his surroundings. He seemed to know his way, as though he had been here before.

He brought the Durlin before the dais and stopped. His gaze was fixed on Ginsar, but once it flickered briefly to Gil. Gil could read nothing of what was to come in that look.

"Welcome to my realm," Ginsar said. Her voice was deep and resonant. "Have I not a beautiful throne room? Fairer by far than that hovel in Cardoroth."

Brand looked around momentarily, taking in the rubbish, the ruin and the debris of long-ago floods. A slight frown marked his face, and Gil knew that he had just realized that Ginsar was insane. But Brand said nothing of it.

"I've been here before," he said. "It's not much different."

Ginsar stood, and she took a grip of Gil's arm. Her fingers tightened into his flesh like steel pincers, and he realized that she was much stronger than she looked.

"Yes. You have been here before," she repeated. "But things will go harder for you this time than they did then."

"As I recall, they were not easy the first time."

Gil did not understand what they were talking about. Something else had happened in this chamber once, but he had no idea what it was.

Brand looked at Ginsar closely. "I was here that day, the day of which you speak, but you were not."

"No. No I was not. And lucky for you."

Brand considered her quietly for a moment, then spoke in his usual direct manner.

"What is your grudge against me? We have not met."

Ginsar laughed, but her eyes flared with the cold light that always burned in them.

"You," she said, stretching forth her long arm, "killed a man. You killed him, here in this underground sanctuary, just a little behind me in the great treasure chamber." She gestured imperiously with a finger to the tapestry-covered wall behind her, but did not take her gaze from him. "I'm sure you remember the way."

Brand looked at her a long time. "Now I know. A man died here. Others too. Good men, some of them. But the one you speak of was called Felargin. Yet he was a sorcerer, and he would have killed us."

"But you killed him instead!"

Brand shrugged. "He brought it on himself. He did a wicked thing, and he betrayed us. He would have given us over to a fate worse than death. I have no regret for my actions that day."

Brand, forthright as ever, returned her gaze steadily.

182

"Who was he to you?"

"My brother."

The chamber was silent. Ginsar and Brand held each other's gazes, unflinching. Gil shifted uneasily, but the grip of the sorceress tightened further on his arm and he stilled. At least there seemed no chance that the two of them had conspired together. It may be that Brand had never betrayed him at all.

At length, Brand spoke. "And this now is revenge? Your brother was evil. I wish that none of that had happened, but I did no wrong. The wrong was his, and now it is yours."

Gil feared an outburst from Ginsar, but instead she only smiled at Brand as though he said the very thing that she wanted him to.

"You know so well what is right and wrong? Then I will give you a choice. And in the choosing you shall reveal what manner of man you are." She squeezed Gil's arm even harder, but he refused to show any pain.

"I hate you," she continued. "And I hate the boy. He is descended from Carnhaina, and I hate *her* most of all. She destroyed my people, stole away our glory in battles long before either of you were born."

Ginsar looked at Brand and her gaze was fierce and exultant. This now was her moment, and Gil realized that it was what she had been waiting for all along.

"Know this!" she said, and the cold fire in her eyes now filled her voice. "Revenge is sweet upon my tongue, but even in victory I show you mercy. See! I will make you this offer. Leave, and become king of Cardoroth. Or stay and perish. So easy, Brand. Betray and live, or remain loyal and die."

"And the boy?"

"It is the same for him. One choice brings life, another death. But I give only you the power of choosing. Your life is his death, his life is yours."

She looked at him with glee, but Brand's expression did not change. Still, there was a sense of danger about him.

"I and the Durlin are not powerless here."

She laughed. "No, but that too is a choice. Should you try to rescue him I will still his beating heart. Even now my will is bent upon it."

Brand considered that. "And how do I know that you will keep this bargain, if we make it?"

Ginsar pursed her red lips. "I swear it upon he who was my master. My soul belongs to him. Let him claim it, let death take me. Let the dark magic that gives me life spin me into the void if I lie! But only this day, one of you may walk free. Tomorrow, well, that is different."

Brand's eyes bored into hers. There was no indication of what he was thinking.

"And the Durlin?"

She shrugged. "They are nothing to me. They can go."

Gil did not understand exactly what was happening. But he sensed another presence nearby. The realization came to him slowly. He looked around the chamber, but he saw nothing except shadows. Yet his instincts warned him that something was coming.

Ginsar tossed her hair impatiently. "Have you made your choice?"

"I have," Brand answered.

"Then I summon one who will extract its price from you. You, or the boy. And know, all gathered here, that he who comes cannot be defeated."

The shadows in the chamber thickened and cold seeped up from the ground on tendrils of twisting mist.

The torches guttered, but the light in Ginsar's eyes burned all the brighter.

"Choose!" she yelled. And then her laugh came wild and free until the vast chamber echoed with the sound of it.

Eventually, silence returned. But in that quiet, another noise began. It came from without. Gil knew it was the thing that he had sensed before. But now, he could put a name to it. Everything was coming together. Everything was beginning to make sense. But nothing was right, nor ever would be again.

22. Grace

Death entered. He came upon a black horse, and his white robes shimmered about his body. His cowl, white also, shadowed his face. But Gil had seen the visage it hid. He had looked into those eyes from atop the Cardurleth when the horseman had come to the city gate. He had looked, and he wished that he had not.

The black horse snorted, and curls of fire reddened its flaring nostrils. Then, at its master's urging, it picked its way down the slope of rubble. Dust lifted into the air. The cold mist swirled and eddied. The earth itself seemed to groan with the rush and tumble of debris stirred by the horse's coming.

Death came to the bottom of the slope. His mount pranced slowly over the now-level ground, a puff of dust rising from each fall of its dark hooves. Those hooves were shod with metal, and the muffled clang of iron against stone throbbed through the chamber.

The horseman proceeded slowly. Down the aisle of statues he came, riding tall and still as a statue himself, though his mount shook its head and strained at the bit. He was close now, close enough that Gil could see the flies that swarmed and buzzed about him, close enough to smell putrification.

A sword was in Death's hand, sickle-shaped and wicked. The naked blade gleamed, and though the metal was black, unearthly lights glimmered along its length.

The great horse came to a rattling stop and snorted. It was a big animal, all wild and untamed, too big and too alive to be in this chamber.

With a heave, Death leapt from his mount and landed on the floor. The ground trembled. Mist curled up like steam beneath his black boots.

The strange blade hung loosely at his side. But very slowly he raised it up before his face. Then he licked its cold, gleaming length.

Ginsar looked at Brand and spoke, and her voice was crisp with urgency.

"Choose!" she commanded. "Fight what cannot be fought, and die. Or leave the boy in your stead, and return to Cardoroth as king!"

Gil felt cold as ice. In those words he heard the pronouncement of his doom. No man could fight Death and win. No man would dare, not even Brand.

He straightened. So be it. He could not blame Brand. But in the face of such cruel destiny, the pride of kings from which he was born stirred his blood to life. He would not cringe. He would not beg for mercy. He would not allow Ginsar that satisfaction.

Brand turned to look at the dark lady. Finally, there was an emotion on his face. It was resignation. After a long silence, he spoke.

"You are a fool," he said softly to Ginsar. "I made my choice long ago, and I will accept the consequences. You understand nothing, if you do not understand that."

He turned to the men of Cardoroth. "Durlin!" he said. "You will stay out of this. You cannot help, only die. Trust in me, for this is the way it was meant to be. I have known this for a while." He paused, gathering his thoughts. "Protect Gil when I am gone, that is your charge. Do not fear, for the sorceress will keep her word. She has sworn by the magic that gives her life, and she must let you go, or die. And she is not ready for that, nor will ever be."

He looked at Taingern and Shorty. "That is my last command. Do not dishonor me by disobeying. Look now to Gil – he will need you after this."

Brand turned to face Death. He cast away the cloth that covered the object in his left hand. It was a staff. It was his lòhren's staff, so seldom seen. With his right hand he drew his Halathrin-wrought blade. This would be a contest of both magic and cold steel.

Gil felt a lump in his throat. He could not believe what was happening. Death and Carnhaina had both prophesied Brand would die unless he took the throne of Cardoroth. Those prophecies were no longer mere words; the proof of them was come to fruition within this chamber. And Brand had chosen death over betrayal. He would give his life so that Gil might live, and Gil felt a slow tide of shame creep over him at the doubts that he had harbored. But the blood of Carnhaina that ran through his veins began to sing.

The two combatants squared off. Death bowed, long and slow and deep.

"You know that you will die," Death said, and his voice seemed to rise from the earth itself.

"All men die," Brand answered simply.

The two of them faced each other. Death stood erect, a massive figure, broad of shoulder and seemingly solid and invulnerable as the earth. But he was no man; he was a force immutable as the passing of time. Brand was smaller, more vulnerable for all his poise, his head lowered but his breathing slow and steady.

Death struck first. Swift as thought his sickle-shaped sword sliced through the air. It hissed. The dark blade flared with cold light. Brand, barely seeming to move, raised his sword in answer. The two blades clashed. Steel screamed and sparks showered through the shadowy air.

The combatants gave no ground. They struck at each other after that again and again, moving, shifting, transforming from defense to attack and attack to defense in a seamless dance.

Dust fell from the high ceiling. Mist eddied over the floor. The echo of the battle was as ten men fighting, and it thrummed through the chamber, rolled through the isle of statues and vented through the mouth of the cave into the world beyond.

But for the two combatants the world had disappeared. All that existed was their enemy and the ebb and flow of battle, the chances of life and death.

Gil had never seen anything like it. He did not think anyone had. Here, in both adversaries, was great strength combined with blinding speed. Death was the stronger, but just as quick. Yet Brand had the greater skill.

The regent's blade cut, parried and stabbed. Ever it moved with swift and adroit skill, deflecting all attacks and delivering its own venomous strikes. And some of those struck true.

Death had been cut. He had been stabbed. The flies that formed a cloud about him hissed angrily. Yet no blood was drawn. He did not slow. He did not show pain. He did not change at all. Death, even as promised, could not be killed.

Yet Brand was slowing. His breathing was quicker. The skill a little less in his muscle-weary arms. Now, the combatants moved around the chamber somewhat more.

Gil realized that this was Brand's doing. There was no retreat, as such, but the extra movement meant fewer strokes and this gave him some opportunity to try to recover.

But Death, unrelenting, sensing his advantage, drove forward in attack. Brand retreated for the first time. Back he stepped into the row of statues. There, tiredness drew an error from him and he stumbled. It was only a slight failing; it merely put him partially off-balance, but Death pounced.

The great sword cut a glittering arc, all black metal and cold fire. It sizzled through the air like a flash of otherworldly lightning. Down it came at Brand's head.

Gil gasped. The world seemed to still. Only the sword moved, and then somehow Brand ducked beneath the blow.

Thunder rumbled through the chamber as the sword smashed into a statue. The sculpture tumbled and fell into a rumbling heap.

Brand, the staff held wide in one hand for balance, and the sword in the other, pivoted and slashed. His Halathrin blade slid full across the abdomen of his opponent. It was a killing blow.

Brand stepped back, his balance regained. Death straightened and turned to face him. The white robes were slit. A great gash was opened in his leathery flesh, and the stench of corruption filled the air. The flies buzzed, and in a cloud they swarmed about the tattered edges of the rent cloth.

But no blood flowed. Instead, maggots crawled through the opening and fell to writhe on the floor.

Brand took another step back. Gil felt Ginsar tremble with excitement at his side. And then Death moved again.

Slowly, he reached up, took hold of the white cowl and tipped it back to reveal his face. Gil saw, even as he had once before from the Cardurleth, that the rider was no living man. Where a face should have been, there was a skull. Tufted hair sprouted from its dome in lank patches. Skin clung tight to bone around the jaw, but hung in loose folds over the sunken cheeks. Maggots squirmed in the eye sockets. Yet those eyes, bubbling pits of horror, still seemed to see and they fixed upon Brand with unwavering hatred.

"I am Death," the creature said in a hollow voice. "My purpose is to kill. I am the Great Dark. I am the Tomb that Welcomes and the Void that Awaits. You cannot kill me, for I am already dead."

Brand leaned upon his staff and the point of the sword in his hand trailed toward the ground.

"That may be," the regent said wearily. "Or it may not. From the Dark you were born. Back into the Dark you can be sent."

"You will learn," Death replied. "I cannot be killed. I have no weakness. None."

Brand did not answer, but the tip of his sword lifted slightly, and a faraway look came into his eyes. He had learned something. Gil was sure of it.

And then Brand took them all by surprise. He attacked, but not with the sword that was already moving. Instead, the staff lifted and thrust forward. Flame burst from it, silver white. It rushed through the air with a roar, and engulfed his opponent. The flies burned away in a spray of sparks. Flame seethed and twisted. Death staggered back, his arm brought up to shield his face. The whole cavern burned with light as though the midday sun had risen from the floor.

191

Brand did not relent. He prodded with the staff. The flames roared louder. Death fell to his knees and the fire burned around him. The dust on the floor turned to ash, and the flagstones beneath glowed red.

At length, Brand's arm trembled. The fire went out and he staggered and fell to his own knees. But there, before him, Death grinned.

Slowly, the creature stood. Wisps of smoke curled from his scorched skin. The tufts of hair were gone and more bone showed. But he seemed unharmed.

"I am Death. I have come. And all the world shall tremble at my feet."

The creature did not even look at Brand. He did not look at Ginsar. Instead, he seemed to be speaking to the world itself.

The Durlin edged forward. Brand raised his head to look at them, particularly Shorty and Taingern.

"No, my friends. Do not jeopardize things. I have already won freedom for Gil."

Brand forced himself to his feet. Death stepped toward him, his sickle-shaped blade raised high. Once more the clash of steel rang through the chamber. But it was no longer the match that it was. Brand was weary now, and yet Death was the same as he had begun.

Yet still Brand landed blows with his sword. And where fire had failed, he summoned cold and wind and darting lights to his opponent's eyes. But neither steel nor lòhrengai had effect.

Death struck blow after blow of his own. On he came, relentless, unyielding, insurmountable. Brand fought bravely, but this was a fight beyond mortal strength. He could not win. He knew that he could not win. Gil finally realized that he had known this from the beginning, yet still he had chosen to fight.

Brand staggered back. Death stalked him. The regent looked to Shorty and Taingern. He gave them the flicker of a sad smile. Then he fixed Death with his gaze. But when he spoke, it was more to his friends.

"You are a force not of this world. You were drawn into the shell of what once was a man, given life for one reason only … to kill me or the boy. Now, I am marked, and I must die. But she who brought you into this world draws on powers beyond the reach of her thought. She does not grasp that she cannot control them. But this I know. Your powers grow, and they will continue to grow as her control lessens. And though you think yourself invincible, there is one way you can be defeated, though it cost me my life."

Brand cast aside both sword and staff, and they rattled against the floor. He stood before his enemy, weaponless. Gil felt his arm grow numb where Ginsar gripped him, and as Brand spoke her fingers sank even deeper into his flesh.

"The magic that called you forth," Brand said, "has a weakness, as all spells must however strong they be. Yours is that you exist to overcome and kill your opponent, for that was the nature of the magic that drew you into this world. You must take life. Thus, you do not weaken no matter how much I fight for mine, for it fulfills your purpose to take it from me." Brand paused, and then spoke slowly. "Yet what if the struggle ceases? I think then that your foothold in this world will diminish, and you can be sent back whence you came."

Brand opened wide his arms. He advanced slowly on Death. "Come! I resist you no longer!"

Brand stepped forward. Death stood, uncertain. But when Brand was within reach Death thrust out with his sword. Or Brand fell upon it. The sickle-shaped blade went right through the regent, and a moment they stood thus.

Brand groaned. Death seemed puzzled, as though surprised that he had struck. And then Brand stiffened. With a shout, he flung himself forward, driving the blade further through his body.

Blood spurted from his back and sprayed over the floor. Yet his hands reached forth, somehow still strong, and they gripped Death's head. There they squeezed, and a silver light flickered at the fingertips.

Death tried to back away. Brand kept his grip. For several long moments they stood together, and then Death screamed and pulled himself free.

He ripped the curved sword from Brand's body, and the regent screamed also. But somehow he kept to his feet. There they faced each other. Death raised high the sword to strike again, but even as he did so, even as he prepared to land the final blow, the strength that was in him withered away.

The sickle-shaped blade fell to the floor with a clatter of steel. The sorcerous light that once infused it was gone. Instead, it glistened with Brand's lifeblood.

A cold wind blew, stirring up dust, tearing apart the mist that rose from the ground, and then it ran through the aisle of statues and moaned as it rushed from the cave mouth.

Death still stood, but he was changed. There was no life in him. The body, held together by sorcery alone, collapsed as the spell that bound it broke.

The once-mighty figure fell to the ground. A foul stench spread through the air. Bones rattled within the white robes and maggots wriggled over the floor.

A moment Brand stood. A moment he regarded the enemy that he had vanquished. And then he also toppled to the floor.

Into the now-silent chamber, Ginsar screamed. Gil ripped free from her grip and ran to Brand. He knelt beside him, and knew that Shorty and Taingern were close by.

Blood seeped from a corner of Brand's mouth. But his eyes were open and they focused on Gil.

"All things have a beginning," the regent whispered to him. "And all things end. As it is in nature … so it is with men." He coughed, and then winced with stabbing pain. "A man must learn to accept death … to face it with grace. Remember that, Gil…"

The regent's voice trailed off. With a sigh, he died, and the light vanished from his eyes. Gil trembled uncontrollably. But it seemed that the whole world around him had gone perfectly still, that it marked the passing of a unique greatness.

He began to sob, but he was roughly pulled away from Brand's body by an elùgroth. Ginsar was there suddenly, and she kicked Brand's corpse. New blood seeped from his wound, and his dagger tumbled from the sheath in his belt, the dagger once given to him by the old king. It lay there on the dirt-crusted floor, next to Brand's lifeless hand. On a finger of that same hand Gil saw the ring that Brand always wore, the very ring given to him by Carnhaina. And on both dagger and ring was the sign of Halathgar.

Ginsar bent down to Gil. "Look on him well, child. He is dead, and you will also die soon. Not today, but maybe tomorrow." She straightened and laughed gaily. "You will not know where I or my allies are, or how we shall strike. But strike we shall. You shall fall. Cardoroth shall fall, and Carnhaina's despairing howls will fill the void!"

She flicked her fingers at him contemptuously, and then strode toward the cave entrance. She paused only to grasp the reins of Death's horse as she passed. The elùgroths filed silently after her, a trail of shadows in her wake.

Gil bowed his head and wept. But soon he felt a hand on his shoulder. It was Taingern.

"They're gone," the Durlindrath said.

Gil looked up. The Durlin surrounded him and Brand's body. There were tears in Taingern's eyes, and also in Shorty's who stood next to him.

"Brand knew," Taingern said. "There was only one way to defeat the creature that the sorceress had called forth. All along he *knew.*

"But how did he do it?" Gil sobbed. "I don't understand."

Taingern knelt beside him. "Brand's every action showed it. And his last act was to voice it. Death cannot be defeated. It cannot be stopped nor banished. But it can be accepted. By acceptance, its power is reduced."

Taingern stood again. The Durlin drew closer. As one they raised their voices in the Durlin creed:

Tum del conar – El dar tum!
Death or infamy – I choose death!

The words drifted away to silence in the vast chamber. And then Shorty and Taingern spoke in unison: *We will not forget him*, they said.

The Durlin gave the ritual reply: *Long will we remember him*.

Gil sobbed anew. Those words were from the Durlin funeral ceremony. He could not believe this was happening. Brand was dead. He was dead, and though Carnhaina had promised she would help him when he needed it most, there had been no sign of her.

He could not stop sobbing. It racked his body and made him tremble. Tears filled his eyes and ran down his cheeks. He could not see clearly. But he could not take his eyes off Brand, and he knew that he would see what he saw now all the days of his life.

Through his blurred vision he saw once more the sign of Halathgar on the signet ring and the dagger. And the twin stars blinked and shimmered back at him, like eyes.

23. I Who Straddle Life and Death

The Durlin were silent now. Gil ceased to sob. He lifted his head and looked at Taingern and Shorty.

"Carnhaina came to me in a dream," he told them. "She warned me – she *warned* me that Brand would need help. She gave me the power to summon her. If only I had done that before!"

Shorty rested a hand on his shoulder. "Don't blame yourself, Gil. Brand knew what he was doing. Only by accepting his death did he weaken that thing, whoever or whatever it was. He had to die to win, and I don't think Carnhaina would have changed that. She warned him of it, after all."

That was true. And yet Gil had a feeling that things were not finished yet. If not before, was now the moment that Carnhaina had told him about? It was too late, and it did not make sense, but the more that he thought about it the more certain he grew that something remained undone.

He looked down again. Carnhaina had told him that he would know how to summon her when the time came. Once more his eyes were drawn to Brand's signet ring and dagger. Again the mark of Halathgar twinkled at him, and like eyes in the dark they watched him. He felt the marks on his palm itch, and finally he understood how to call her forth. In realizing this, he also knew that it was the moment to do so.

"I can do it," he whispered. "And I must."

Shorty and Taingern looked at him strangely. For a moment, they did nothing. Then they signaled the Durlin to stand back, but they did not move themselves.

Gil bent down. Gently, he removed Brand's signet ring. He clenched it tight to the palm of his left hand. In his right, he took a firm grip of the dagger.

Both items were once Carnhaina's. There was magic in them also; he sensed its presence readily enough. But that alone would not suffice to bridge the gap between life and death and summon Carnhaina's spirit to him. More would be needed to connect him to her, and he knew what.

The sign of Halathgar on the two objects touched the marks on his palms. There they tingled, and the magic within them stirred, expectantly. Even as Brand had once told him, it was alive.

He concentrated. The magic pulsed, and he coaxed it forth. The power inside him, the magic that he was born with, sparked to life also. It rose within him, stronger and surer than he had ever felt it. He almost panicked, but he drew the two powers together and mingled them inside himself. Then he gave it focus in the way that he must in order to summon Carnhaina.

He thought of her. He remembered her. Most of all, he opened himself to the way she made him feel. There were no words for that. There were no thoughts. He just allowed the emotions to wash over him, to become one with him and the magic that pulsed to life inside him.

And then there was more than thought and memory and emotion. She was here. He sensed her presence all about him.

He stood up and turned around. She was there, looking at him. But she was not as he had seen her on the tower

199

of Halathgar. Now, she seemed real. There was different magic at work here. Stronger and more dangerous.

She stood, regal as always. The spear was in her hand, the point gleaming with a cold light like stars on a winter's night.

The Durlin edged forward. They did not know who she was, and there was fear on their faces, but it was clear they were prepared to protect Brand's body if they must.

"Leave him!" commanded the queen.

Taingern signaled everyone to step back, and they did so reluctantly.

Carnhaina knelt. With a pale hand, yet one that seemed real rather than ghostly, she touched Brand's cheek.

"Here is one," she said, "who gave much to Alithoras. All, in the end. A hero, and there are few like him. Even in the Age of Heroes, there were few like him…"

"Can you bring him back?" Gil asked. It was the first thought that crossed his mind, however foolish.

The queen used the spear to help her stand again. There was a vast silence after his words, and it seemed that the roof of the chamber pressed down. The Durlin watched, pale-faced and wide-eyed.

"I am Carnhaina. I am mighty in power and learned in lore that would shrivel most souls. Yet that, *that* is beyond even my strength."

Gil dropped his head, but the queen was not done.

"But know this, brave child. Ginsar, in her madness, has opened ways to other worlds. That is whence the Horsemen come. The walls of reality are sundered, and just now, I, who myself have been summoned to this land; I, who straddle life and death; I, one of the great powers of Alithoras, may yet have a chance to recall Brand's spirit and heal his body through the same ways that she herself has opened." Light flickered at the sharp tip of her spear. "Stand back!" she cried, and dust fell from the ceiling as her voice rang in the chamber. "Stand back!"

They all moved. Gil, frightened and in awe of her, staggered away, but Shorty and Taingern were at his side and steadied him. If they were as scared as he, they did not show it.

The queen lifted her arms. Thunder rumbled through the cavern. Dust and ancient plaster fell from the ceiling. The earth screamed as stone ground on stone, and water bubbled through widening gaps in the floor.

Gil's vision swam. When it cleared, it seemed to him that he stood in two places at once. The torch-lit chamber was still around him, but he also saw, as though etched over that, the ice-cracked stone of a high summit beneath his feet. Beyond was the shoulder of a rock-strewn mountain. A long and grassy slope tumbled away before him, leading toward a green valley; and he smelled trees. Pine trees, sharp and fresh.

Brand was there. He lay, dead, upon the floor of the chamber. But he stood in that other place, tall and powerful and alive. A light was in his eyes, and he gazed at Carnhaina who stood before him, her spear raised above her head.

She spoke. Brand answered. But Gil heard nothing of their words. After a moment, the regent lifted high his arms and looked to the sky.

The mountain lurched. The queen pointed at him with her spear and called lightning from the heavens. It struck Brand, searing him, running up and down his body. But he stood still and kept his arms up as though to embrace it.

Back in the chamber, Carnhaina was in the same position, but multicolored flame streamed from the tip of her spear. This was pointed at Brand. The flame enveloped him, and his body trembled.

Thrice she thrust the spear. Thrice Brand's body flinched under the influence of her magic. Gil saw also that atop the mountain she called forth lightning three times. The last was a searing bolt that sizzled through the air, struck Brand, and leaped to the stone near his feet. The rock split. Water gushed through the crack and hastened in a stream down the green slope and into the valley.

In the chamber, the flame flickered out. Brand lay still, but the blood on his clothing was burned away. His chest heaved, and then with a great gasp he gulped in air. His eyes flickered open.

"It is done!" Carnhaina proclaimed. She seemed very weak, and lowered the butt of her spear to the floor so that she could lean on it. "Listen!" she continued. "Ginsar has loosed forces upon the land that tear at reality. Because of her, a way was open for me to return Brand. In her madness, in her lust for revenge, she opened a portal and drew these forces in. She thinks to master them, but they will conquer her instead. And after, they will turn to this fresh world, to every blade of grass, every grain of sand, every day and every night, to every person; and they will make it all their own. That must not be! You must prevent it! You must close the opening that Ginsar has made."

Carnhaina trembled and shut her eyes. When she opened them, she stared straight at Gil.

"How can we close it?" he asked her.

The queen slowly shook her head. "I don't know. I have no idea."

Gil was staggered. He had thought that her knowledge and power was enormous. And so it was, but even such as she had limits.

"But know this," she said. "This quest I set you. It is for this that you were born. Seek the answer, and you will find it."

Her voice trailed away in weariness. Gil would have asked her more but she held up her hand.

"I am spent. Have faith that you will know what to do and how to do it … when the time is right. But you will need to be strong."

With a groan, she fell to her knees. She looked up at him, her eyes piercing bright, willing him to take up the quest, and then she wavered and was gone as though a light had been extinguished.

Gil looked at Brand. The regent still lay on the ground, but he was propped up on one elbow, watching. And those eyes, those intense eyes fixed on him, those same eyes that moments ago had stared at him without life. Now, there was a myriad of emotions in them, too deep and too complex for Gil to understand.

Around them all, the chamber began to rumble violently. The water that gushed through the cracked stone began to hiss and steam.

"Earthquake!" Hruilgar yelled.

All thought of the quest given to Gil was lost. He thought instead of the weight of the earth above him. Even as he did so sheets of plaster and loosened rock began to fall. The earth shook beneath his feet and he stumbled. Brand tried to rise, but fell.

The Durlin moved with speed. While Gil was still caught by fear some of them drew around him and propelled him forward. Others gathered Brand into their arms and lifted him. Then they ran.

Hruilgar led the escape. Sweeping up a torch from the dais into his steady hand, he led them off. Through the aisle of statues he raced, but those statues shuddered and moved about him. Some tumbled to the floor. But nothing stopped either him or the Durlin. They hastened forward, bringing their charges with them, and they came to the slope of rubble.

This was harder. It moved and seethed as the earth shuddered. Yet still Hruilgar found a way up, and the Durlin followed him. Twice those carrying Brand fell, and twice other Durlin lent their strength until they were at the top.

The cave was dark. It shook and rumbled and air hissed through the entrance a little way ahead. They raced for it, striving toward the daylight that they could see and to the open air they knew was beyond.

Behind, the earth groaned and the slope of rubble collapsed into the chamber. A plume of dust rose, choking and thick.

Gil could barely breathe. He saw nothing through the dust-thickened air. Even the daylight at the entrance that moments ago had served as a signpost of escape was gone. All around him massive chunks of stone fell from the ceiling and tumbled to the floor. The sound of it was like drum strokes of doom in his ears.

He coughed and spluttered. The Durlin around him moved. But they moved slowly, as disorientated as he was, and he did not think they knew better than he where the mouth of the cave opened to the outside world.

It was then that he heard a horn. Over the tumult it lifted. A clear sound, a crisp sound. A sound called forth to save them, if they could but heed it in time. It was Hruilgar's hunting horn, and he had found the way out.

Thus ends *Prince of the Magic*. The Son of Sorcery series will continue in Book Two, where Gil will learn more of the threat to Cardoroth and the quest bestowed upon him.

Sign up below and be the first to hear about new book releases, see previews and learn of upcoming discounts. http://eepurl.com/Rswv1

Visit my website at www.homeofhighfantasy.com

Dedication

There's a growing movement in fantasy literature. Its name is noblebright, and it's the opposite of grimdark.

Noblebright celebrates the virtues of heroism. It's an old-fashioned thing, as old as the first story ever told around a smoky campfire beneath ancient stars. It's storytelling that highlights courage and loyalty and hope for the spirit of humanity. It recognizes the dark, the dark in us all, and the dark in the villains of its stories. It recognizes death, and treachery and betrayal. But it dwells on none of those things.

I dedicate this book, such as it is, to that which is noblebright. And I thank the authors before me who held the torch high so that I could see the path: J.R.R. Tolkien, C.S. Lewis, Terry Brooks, David Eddings, Susan Cooper, Roger Taylor and many others. I salute you.

And, for a time, I too will hold the torch as high as I can.

Encyclopedic Glossary

Note: the glossary of each book in this series is individualized for that book alone. Additionally, there is often historical material provided in its entries for people, artifacts and events that are not included in the main text.

Many races dwell in Alithoras. All have their own language, and though sometimes related to one another, the changes sparked by migration, isolation and various influences often render these tongues unintelligible to each other.

The ascendancy of Halathrin culture, combined with their widespread efforts to secure and maintain allies against elug incursions, has made their language the primary means of communication between diverse peoples.

For instance, a soldier of Cardoroth addressing a ship's captain from Camarelon would speak Halathrin, or a simplified version of it, even though their native speeches stem from the same ancestral language.

This glossary contains a range of names and terms. Many are of Halathrin origin, and their meaning is provided. The remainder derive from native tongues and are obscure, so meanings are only given intermittently.

Some variation exists within the Halathrin language, chiefly between the regions of Halathar and Alonin. The most obvious example is the latter's preference for a "dh" spelling instead of "th".

Often, Camar names and Halathrin elements are combined. This is especially so for the aristocracy. No other tribes of men had such long-term friendship with the immortal Halathrin, and though in this relationship they lost some of their natural culture, they gained nobility and knowledge in return.

List of abbreviations:

Azn. Azan

Cam. Camar

Comb. Combined

Cor. Corrupted form

Duth. Duthenor

Esg. Esgallien

Hal. Halathrin

Leth. Letharn

Prn. Pronounced

Age of Heroes: A period of Camar history, which has become mythical. Many tales are told of this time. Some are true, others are not. And yet, even the false ones usually contain elements of historical fact. Many were the heroes who walked abroad during this time, and they are remembered still, and honored still, by the Camar people. The old days are looked back on with pride, and the descendants of many heroes yet walk the streets of Cardoroth, though they be unaware of their heritage and the accomplishments of their forefathers.

Alithoras: *Hal.* "Silver land." The Halathrin name for the continent they settled after their exodus from their homeland. Refers to the extensive river and lake systems they found and their appreciation of the beauty of the land.

Anast Dennath: *Hal.* "Stone mountains." Mountain range in northern Alithoras. Contiguous with Auren Dennath.

Arach Neben: *Hal.* "West gate." The great wall surrounding Cardoroth has four gates. Each is named after a cardinal direction, and each also carries a token to represent a celestial object. Arach Neben bears a steel ornament of the Morning Star.

Arell: Rumored to be Brand's mistress. A name formerly common among the Camar people, but currently out of favor in Cardoroth. Its etymology is obscure, though it is speculated that it derives from the Halathrin stems "aran" and "ell" meaning noble and slender. Ell, in the Halathrin tongue, also refers to any type of timber that is pliable, for instance, hazel. This is cognate with our word wych-wood, meaning timber that is supple and pliable. As elùgroths use wych-wood staffs as instruments of sorcery, it is sometimes supposed that their name derives from this stem, rather than elù (shadowed). This is a viable philological theory. Nevertheless, as a matter of historical fact, it is wrong.

Aurellin: *Cor. Hal.* The first element means blue. The second appears to be native Camar. Queen of Cardoroth, wife to Gilhain and grandmother to Gilcarist.

Auren Dennath: *Comb. Duth.* and *Hal. Prn.* Our-ren dennath. "Blue mountains." Mountain range in northern Alithoras. Contiguous with Anast Dennath.

Brand: A Duthenor tribesman. Appointed by the former king of Cardoroth to serve as regent for Gilcarist. By birth, he is the rightful chieftain of the Duthenor people. However, a usurper overthrew his father, killing him and his wife. Brand, only a youth at the time, swore an oath of vengeance. That oath sleeps, but it is not forgotten, either by Brand or the usurper.

Camar: *Cam. Prn.* Kay-mar. A race of interrelated tribes that migrated in two main stages. The first brought them to the vicinity of Halathar; in the second, they separated and establish cities along a broad sweep of eastern Alithoras.

Camarelon: *Cam. Prn.* Kam-arelon. A port city and capital of a Camar tribe. It was founded before Cardoroth as the waves of migrating people settled the more southerly lands first. Each new migration tended northward. It is perhaps the most representative of a traditional Camar realm.

Cardoroth: *Cor. Hal. Comb. Cam.* A Camar city, often called Red Cardoroth. Some say this alludes to the red granite commonly used in the construction of its buildings, others that it refers to a prophecy of destruction.

Cardurleth: *Hal.* "Car – red, dur – steadfast, leth – stone." The great wall that surrounds Cardoroth. Established soon after the city's founding and constructed with red granite. It looks displeasing to the eye, but the people of the city love it nonetheless. They believe it impregnable and say that no enemy shall ever breach it – except by treachery.

Careth Nien: *Hal. Prn.* Kareth nyen. "Great river." Largest river in Alithoras. Has its source in the mountains of Anast Dennath and runs southeast across the land before emptying into the sea. It was over this river (which sometimes freezes along its northern stretches) that the Camar and other tribes migrated into the eastern lands. Much later, Brand came to the city of Cardoroth by one of these ancient migratory routes.

Carnhaina: First element native *Cam.* Second *Hal.* "Heroine." An ancient queen of Cardoroth. Revered as a savior of her people, but to some degree also feared for she possessed powers of magic. Hated to this day by elùgroths, because she overthrew their power unexpectedly at a time when their dark influence was rising. According to dim legend, kept alive mostly within the royal family of Cardoroth, she guards the city even in death and will return in its darkest hour.

Chapterhouse: Special halls set aside in the palace of Cardoroth for the private meetings, teachings and military training of the Durlin.

Dernbrael: *Hal.* "Sharp tongued, or by some translations, cunning tongued." A lord of Cardoroth. Out of favor with the old king due to mistrust. It is said that he is in league with the traitor Hvargil, though this has never been proven. It is known, however, that Hvargil once saved his life when they were younger men. This occurred in a gambling den of ill-repute, and the details are obscure. Nevertheless, all accounts agree that Hvargil was wounded protecting his friend.

Durlin: *Hal.* "The steadfast." The original Durlin were the seven sons of the first king of Cardoroth. They guarded him against all enemies, of which there were many, and three died to protect him. Their tradition continued throughout Cardoroth's history, suspended only once, and briefly, some four hundred years ago when it was discovered that three members were secretly in the service of elùgroths. These were imprisoned, but committed suicide while waiting for the king's trial to commence. It is rumored that the king himself provided them with the knives that they used. It is said that he felt sorry for them and gave them this way out to avoid the shame a trial would bring to their families.

Durlin creed: These are the native Camar words, long remembered and much honored, uttered by the first Durlin to die while he defended his father, and king, from attack. Tum del conar – El dar tum! Death or infamy – I choose death!

Durlindrath: *Hal.* "Lord of the steadfast." The title given to the leader of the Durlin. For the first time in the history of Cardoroth, that esteemed position is held jointly by two people: Lornach and Taingern. Lornach also possesses the title of King's Champion. The latter honor is not held in quite such high esteem, yet it carries somewhat more power. As King's Champion, Lornach is authorized to act in the king's stead in matters of honor and treachery to the Crown.

Duthenor: *Duth. Prn.* Dooth-en-or. "The people." A single tribe, or sometimes a group of tribes melded into a larger people at times of war or disaster, who generally live a rustic and peaceful lifestyle. They are raisers of cattle and herders of sheep. However, when need demands they are fierce warriors – men and women alike.

Elrika: *Cam.* Daughter of the royal baker. Friend of Gilcarist, and highly skilled in swordcraft. Brand has given instructions to Lornach that she is to be taught all arts of the warrior to the full extent of her ability. He is to groom her as the first female Durlin in the history of the city.

Elùgrune: *Hal.* Literally "shadowed fortune," but has other meanings such as "ill fortune" and "born of the dark." In the first two senses it is often used to mean simply bad luck. In the third, it describes a person steeped in shadow and mystery and not to be trusted. Also, in some circles, the term is used for a mystic.

Elugs: *Hal.* "That which creeps in shadows." A cruel and superstitious race that inhabits the southern lands, especially the Graèglin Dennath.

Elùdrath: *Hal. Prn.* Eloo-drath. "Shadowed lord." A sorcerer. First and greatest among elùgroths. Believed by most to be dead.

Elùgai: *Hal. Prn.* Eloo-guy. "Shadowed force." The sorcery of an elùgroth.

Elùgroth: *Hal. Prn.* Eloo-groth. "Shadowed horror." A sorcerer. They often take names in the Halathrin tongue in mockery of the lòhren practice to do so.

Elu-haraken: *Hal.* "The shadowed wars." Long ago battles in a time that is become myth to the Camar tribes.

Esanda: No known etymology for this name. Likewise, Esanda herself is not originally from Cardoroth. The old king believed she was from the city of Esgallien, but he was not certain of this. Esanda herself refuses to answer any questions about her origins. Notwithstanding the personal mystery surrounding her, she was one of the old king's most trusted advisors and soon became so to Brand. She heads a ring of spies devoted to the protection of Cardoroth from its many enemies.

Esgallien: *Hal. Prn.* Ez-gally-en. "Es – rushing water, gal(en) – green, lien – to cross: place of the crossing onto the green plains." A city established in antiquity and named after a nearby ford of the Careth Nien.

Felargin: *Cam.* A sorcerer. Brother to Ginsar. Acolyte of Shurilgar, Betrayer of Nations. Steeped in evil and once lured Brand, Shorty and others under false pretenses into a quest. Only Brand and Shorty survived the betrayal. Felargin himself suffered the doom he had prepared for his victims, and it was a fate worse than death.

Fereck: *Cam.* The royal farrier. Emigrated a great distance from Esgallien but soon found employment in the palace of Cardoroth due to his great skill. A quiet and thoughtful man, and one from whom Brand sometimes seeks advice.

Foresight: Premonition of the future. Can occur at random as a single image or as a longer sequence of events. Can also be deliberately sought by entering the realm between life and death where the spirit is released from the body to travel through space and time. To achieve this, the body must be brought to the very threshold of death. The first method is uncontrollable and rare. The second exceedingly rare but controllable for those with the skill and willingness to endure the danger.

Forgotten Queen (the): An epithet of Queen Carnhaina. She was a person of immense power and presence, yet she made few friends in life, and her possession of magic made her mistrusted. For these reasons, memory of her accomplishments faded soon after her death and only snatches of her rule are remembered by the populace of Cardoroth. Yet the history books record a far fuller description of her queenship.

Gil: See Gilcarist.

Gilcarist: *Comb. Cam & Hal.* First element unknown, second "ice." Heir to the throne of Cardoroth and grandson of King Gilhain. According to Carnhaina, his coming was told in the stars. He is The Star-marked One, The Boy with Two Fates, The Guarded and the Hunted, The King Who Might Rule, The Lòhren Who Might Teach, The Boy Who Might Live and the Boy Who Might Die. He is also foretold as The Savior and the Destroyer. But these names meaning nothing to him, and he prefers to follow Brand's view that a man makes his own fate.

Gilhain: *Comb. Cam & Hal.* First element unknown, second "hero." King of Cardoroth before proclaiming Brand regent for the heir to the throne. Husband to Aurellin.

Ginsar: *Cam.* A sorceress. Sister to Felargin. Acolyte of Shurilgar, Betrayer of Nations. Steeped in evil and greatly skilled in the arts of elùgai, reaching a level of proficiency nearly as great as her master.

Goblins: See elugs.

Graèglin Dennath: *Hal. Prn.* Greg-lin dennath. "Mountains of ash." Chain of mountains in southern Alithoras. The landscape is one of jagged stone and boulder, relieved only by gaping fissures from which plumes of ashen smoke ascend, thus leading to its name. Believed to be impassable because of the danger of poisonous air flowing from cracks, and the ground unexpectedly giving way, swallowing any who dare to tread its forbidden paths. In other places swathes of molten stone run in rivers down its slopes.

Grothanon: *Hal.* "Horror desert." The flat salt plains south of the Graèglin Dennath.

Halathar: *Hal.* "Dwelling place of the people of Halath." The forest realm of the Halathrin.

Halathgar: *Hal.* "Bright star." Actually a constellation of two stars. Also known as the Lost Huntress.

Halathrin: *Hal.* "People of Halath." A race named after a mighty lord who led an exodus of his people to the continent of Alithoras in pursuit of justice, having sworn to redress a great evil. They are human, though of fairer

217

form, greater skill and higher culture than ordinary men. They possess an inherent unity of body, mind and spirit enabling insight and endurance beyond other races of Alithoras. Reported to be immortal, but killed in great numbers during their conflicts with the evil they seek to destroy. Those conflicts are collectively known as the Elùharaken: the Shadowed Wars.

Harath Neben: *Hal.* "North gate." This gate bears a token of two massive emeralds that represent the constellation of Halathgar. The gate is also known as "Hunter's Gate," for the north road out of the city leads to wild lands full of game.

Hruilgar: *Comb. Cam & Hal.* First element unknown (but thought to mean "wild"), second "star." The king's huntsman. Rumored to have learned his craft as a tracker in Esgallien and to have come northward at the same time as Sandy.

Hvargil: Prince of Cardoroth. Younger son of Carangil, former king of Cardoroth. Exiled by Carangil for treason after it was discovered he plotted with elùgroths to assassinate his older half-brother, Gilhain, and prevent him from one day ascending the throne. He gathered a band about him in exile of outlaws and discontents. Most came from Cardoroth but others were drawn from Camarelon. In confirmation of his treachery, he fought with an invading army against his own homeland in the recent war.

Immortals: See Halathrin.

Lake Alithorin: *Hal.* "Silver lake." A lake of northern Alithoras.

Lòhren: *Hal. Prn.* Ler-ren. "Knowledge giver – a counsellor." Other terms used by various nations include wizard, druid and sage.

Lòhren-fire: A defensive manifestation of lòhrengai. The color of the flame varies according to the skill and temperament of the lòhren.

Lòhrengai: *Hal. Prn.* Ler-ren-guy. "Lòhren force." Enchantment, spell or use of arcane power. A manipulation and transformation of the natural energy inherent in all things. Each use takes something from the user. Likewise, some part of the transformed energy infuses them. Lòhrens use it sparingly, elùgroths indiscriminately.

Lòrenta: *Hal. Prn.* Ler-rent-a. "Hills of knowledge." Uplands in northern Alithoras in which the stronghold of the lòhrens is established. It is to here that the old king and queen of Cardoroth traveled to spend the last years of the lives in peace after their service to the realm.

Lornach: *Cam.* A former Durlin and now joint Durlindrath. Friend to Brand and often called by his nickname of "Shorty."

Lost Huntress: See Halathgar.

Magic: Supernatural power. See lòhrengai and elùgai.

Nightborn: See elùgrune.

Otherworld: Camar term for a mingling of half-remembered history, myth and the spirit world. Sometimes used interchangeably with the term "Age of Heroes."

Sandy: See Esanda.

Sellic Neben: *Hal.* "East gate." This gate bears a representation, crafted of silver and pearl, of the moon rising over the sea.

Shadowed Lord: See Elùdrath.

Shorty: See Lornach.

Shurilgar: *Hal.* "Midnight star." An elùgroth. One of the most puissant sorcerers of antiquity. Known to legend as the Betrayer of Nations.

Sight: The ability to discern the intentions and even thoughts of another person. Not reliable, and yet effective at times.

Spirit walk: Similar in process to foresight. It is deliberately sought by entering the realm between life and death where the spirit is released from the body to travel through space. To achieve this, the body must be brought to the very threshold of death. This is exceedingly dangerous and only attempted by those of paramount skill.

Sorcerer: See Elùgroth.

Sorcery: See elùgai.

Surcoat: An outer garment. Often worn over chain mail. The Durlin surcoat is unadorned white, which is a tradition carried down from the order's inception.

Swordmaster: A title bestowed by the King of Cardoroth. It comes with obligations, the most well-known of which is the tuition of gifted youths in the art of sword fighting. In ancient times, it was held to be a high honor and there were often several appointed at one time. In the later days of Cardoroth, the tradition has diminished to more of an honorary role.

Taingern: *Cam.* A former Durlin. Friend to Brand, and now joint Durlindrath. Once, in company of Brand, saved the tomb of Carnhaina from defilement and robbery by an elùgroth.

Torc: A neck ring, either of multiple strands of gold twisted together or one thick strand. A symbol of authority and power in ancient Camar society. The most resplendent ever made once adorned Queen Carnhaina herself, and it was interred with her as was customary in Camar tradition.

Tower of Halathgar: In life, the place of study of Queen Carnhaina. In death, her resting place. Somewhat unusually, her sarcophagus rests on the tower's parapet beneath the stars.

Turlak: A youth of Cardoroth city and scion of a noble house. Favored pupil of the Swordmaster.

Unlach Neben: *Hal.* "South gate." This gate bears a representation of the sun, crafted of gold, beating down upon a desert land. Said by some to signify the homeland of the elugs, whence the gold of the sun was obtained by an adventurer of old.

Witch Queen: See Carnhaina

Wizard: See lòhren.

Wych-wood: A general description for a range of supple and springy timbers. Some hardy varieties are prevalent on the poisonous slopes of the Graèglin Dennath mountain range and are favored by elùgroths as instruments of sorcery.

About the author

I'm a man born in the wrong era. My heart yearns for faraway places and even further afield times. Tolkien had me at the beginning of *The Hobbit* when he said, ". . . one morning long ago in the quiet of the world . . ."

Sometimes I imagine myself in a Viking mead-hall. The long winter night presses in, but the shimmering embers of a log in the hearth hold back both cold and dark. The chieftain calls for a story, and I take a sip from my drinking horn and stand up . . .

Or maybe the desert stars shine bright and clear, obscured occasionally by wisps of smoke from burning camel dung. A dry gust of wind marches sand grains across our lonely campsite, and the wayfarers about me stir restlessly. I sip cool water and begin to speak.

I'm a storyteller. A man to paint a picture by the slow music of words. I like to bring faraway places and times to life, to make hearts yearn for something they can never have, unless for a passing moment.

Printed in Poland
by Amazon Fulfillment
Poland Sp. z o.o., Wrocław